WORSHIPERS' MASKS:
THE HIDDEN FACES OF SUCCESS

ONESIMUS MALATJI

Worshipers' Masks: The Hidden Faces of Success
By: Onesimus Malatji

Third-Party Content:

This book may reference or include content from third-party sources. The author and publisher do not endorse or take responsibility for the accuracy or content of such third-party material.

Endorsements:

Any endorsement, testimonial, or representation contained in this book reflects the author's personal views and opinions. It does not imply an endorsement by any third party.
Results Disclaimer: The success stories and examples mentioned in this book are not guarantees of individual success. Actual results may vary based on various factors, including effort and circumstances.

Results Disclaimer:

The success stories and examples mentioned in this book are not guarantees of individual success. Actual results may vary based on various factors, including effort and circumstances.
No Guarantee of Outcome: The strategies, techniques, and advice provided in this book are based on the author's experiences and research. However, there is no guarantee that following these strategies will lead to a specific outcome or result.

Fair Use Notice:

This book may contain copyrighted material used for educational and illustrative purposes. Such material is used under the "fair use" provisions of copyright law.

DEDICATION

Being one of the difficulties in my family, always stubborn, I thank God I turned out alright. I dedicate this book to my mother, Esther Malatji. I will always love you. You have raised me well until I became a fully grown man. Thank you for your prayers and support during my tough times in life. Additionally, I extend my heartfelt dedication to my beautiful wife, the partner of my life, Petunia. You have been there for me and our family, and you are truly one in a million – the best motivator. I thank God for having you as my spouse, partner, and my inspiration; you are one of my most special and wonderful gifts. During times of trials, you have never walked out on us. Thank you. I love you so much.

I also send this dedication to my brother Edward "Gong," one of the greatest creative businesspersons alive. Thank you for being a wonderful brother and supporting me in times of need and trial. May God bless you and increase your business anointing. I love you so much. Special greetings to my sister Bertha, your passion for food will undoubtedly touch the world. I love you.

Furthermore, I extend my love and dedication to my brother Mohau; I will always cherish you, brother. Special Dedication for Galetsang & Dineo I will always love you no matter what. This is also for my friends, and fellow soldiers in war: Zama, Panana, Fina, Tshwane, Blessing, Lowen, Neo, Sile, Judy, Winners I love you guys – you are my family. Special Gratitude to my inspirer my mother. I deeply respect the gift that God has put in you, and I am immensely grateful for having you while I was putting this book together.

Thank you, my dear mother, Esther Malatji. I love you so much

ACKNOWLEDGMENTS

I extend my deepest gratitude to everyone who has been a part of this incredible journey, both seen and unseen. Your support, encouragement, and unwavering belief in me have been the driving force behind the creation of this book.

To my family, for standing by me through thick and thin, for believing in my dreams, and for being a constant source of inspiration – your love and encouragement have been my guiding light.

To my friends, mentors, and colleagues, your valuable insights and feedback have shaped the ideas within these pages. Your willingness to share your wisdom and experiences has enriched this work beyond measure.

To all those who have supported me on my path, whether through a kind word, a helping hand, or a moment of shared understanding, thank you. Your presence in my life has made all the difference.

To the countless individuals who have faced challenges and setbacks, yet continued to strive for greatness, your stories have fuelled the inspiration behind these words. May you find solace and encouragement within these pages.

And finally, to the readers who have embarked on this journey with me, thank you for allowing me to share my thoughts and experiences. It is my hope that this book serves as a beacon of hope, a source of guidance, and a reminder that fulfilment can be found in every step of life's intricate tapestry.

With heartfelt appreciation,

Onesimus Malatji

WORSHIPERS' MASKS:
THE HIDDEN FACES OF SUCCESS

The dream begins in Johannesburg 10-25

Crossing paths in Pretoria 26-40

Triumphs and trial 41-60

Shadows in Cape Town 62-89

Reflections in the storm 91-101

Return to Johannesburg: a changed perspective 102-123

The unmasking 124-132

Rebuilding amongst the ruins 134-176

Epilogue: the journey continues 177-188

Thank You, Letter, From The Author 189-190

WORSHIPERS' MASKS:
THE HIDDEN FACES OF SUCCESS

PART 1: THE ASCENT

THE DREAM BEGINS IN JOHANNESBURG

In the heart-woven streets of Soweto, a suburb pulsating with the vibrant rhythm of Johannesburg, life was a mosaic of vivid colours, spirited conversations, and the unyielding pulse of ambition. Here, among the bustling markets, the laughter of children playing soccer in narrow alleys, and the aroma of braai drifting through the air, lived Thabo, a beacon of youthful ambition and determination.

Thabo's world was one where dreams were as tangible as the red earth beneath his feet. Raised in a community rich in history and resilience, he was a tapestry of his surroundings – embodying the relentless spirit and diverse cultures that thrived amidst the city's complexities. His early life in Soweto was not just about survival, but about finding a voice in the chorus of the city's many stories.

From a young age, Thabo stood apart from his peers. Where others saw limitations, he saw ladders to climb. His eyes, bright with the gleam of possibility, mirrored the city's skyline – always reaching upwards. Thabo was not just another dreamer; he was a planner, a thinker, a doer. His aspirations stretched beyond the confines of his neighbourhood, aiming for the stars that dotted the vast South African sky.

His personality was a blend of charismatic charm and quiet resolve. In the lively debates at the local spaza shop, Thabo's voice was one that resonated with conviction and intelligence. He was a listener, absorbing the wisdom of the elders, the aspirations of his peers, and the lessons hidden in everyday life. He carried within him a deep respect for his roots and a burning desire to carve out a path that would lead him to greatness.

Thabo dreamed of success not just as a personal triumph, but as a beacon of hope for his community. He envisioned creating opportunities not just for himself but for those around him. His dreams were interlaced with a sense of duty – a duty to uplift, to inspire, to change the narrative that the world often wrote for places like Soweto.

Yet, even in his most ambitious daydreams, Thabo remained grounded in the realities of his world. He knew the road to success was paved with challenges, that for every cheer there would be a chorus of doubts, and for every step forward, there might be stumbles. But in his heart, fuelled by the spirit of his homeland, lay an unshakeable belief – the belief that he, Thabo, could be a catalyst for change, a testament to the power of dreams born in the heart of Johannesburg.

Johannesburg: a city of stark contrasts and vibrant energy, a place where dreams are both made and tested. It's a metropolis that pulses with the heartbeat of South Africa, a rhythm composed of diverse cultures, relentless ambition, and the enduring spirit of its people.

The city's skyline, a jagged line of towering skyscrapers, stands as a testament to Johannesburg's economic might and its role as the gold-studded heart of the country. Below these towering giants, the streets thrum with life – a symphony of hooting taxis, street vendors selling colourful wares, and businessmen and women striding purposefully, their ambitions as tall as the buildings under which they walk.

But Johannesburg is not just a city of corporate giants and bustling commerce. It is a tapestry woven with the threads of multiple cultures. In neighbourhoods like Maboneng and Newtown, art and creativity bloom amidst urban renewal, telling stories of a city that constantly reinvents itself. Here, graffiti murals splash walls with vibrant hues, and the sounds of marimba bands blend with the aroma of African spices and street food, creating an ambiance that is uniquely Jozi.

Yet, this city is also one of contrasts. The opulence of Sandton, with its glossy high-rise buildings and luxurious shopping centres, stands in sharp contrast to the makeshift homes in informal settlements like Alexandra, just a stone's throw away. These disparities speak volumes of the challenges that face many of its residents – challenges of inequality, unemployment, and the daily grind to make ends meet.

In the sprawling suburbs, each with its own character, from the leafy streets of Parkhurst to the energetic buzz of Braamfontein, the city's diversity is on full display. It's a place where different languages fill the air, from isiZulu and Sesotho to English and Afrikaans, each adding to the rich tapestry of Johannesburg's identity.

For ambitious souls like Thabo, Johannesburg is not just a backdrop but a character in its own right. It's a place that offers both the highest of highs and the lowest of lows. The city sets the stage for a journey of ambition, where success is not just a destination but a path fraught with obstacles and opportunities, a path that tests the resilience and determination of those who dare to walk it.

In Johannesburg, every street corner, every skyline view, every face in the crowd tells a story. And for those who listen closely, these stories whisper the truths about ambition, success, and the human spirit's relentless pursuit of greatness. Thabo's story is deeply rooted in the fabric of his family, a cornerstone of his identity and ambition. Born into a family that was a microcosm of Johannesburg itself – diverse, resilient, and rich in stories – Thabo's early life was a tapestry of lessons learned around the dinner table and in the daily struggles and triumphs of his kin.

His father, Mandla, was a man of few words but many dreams. A taxi driver who navigated the bustling streets of Jozi, Mandla's hands were as firm on the steering wheel as his beliefs in hard work and perseverance. Each evening, he returned home with stories of the city – tales of diverse passengers, each with their own dreams and struggles, which he shared with his family. These stories were not just anecdotes; they were life lessons about the resilience and determination needed to survive in a city like Johannesburg.

Thabo's mother, Nomsa, was the heart of the home. A nurse at a local clinic, her days were long and demanding, yet she always managed to keep a warm, nurturing atmosphere in their modest Soweto home. It was from her that Thabo learned compassion and the importance of community. Nomsa often shared stories of her patients, teaching Thabo that success was not just about personal achievement, but also about lifting others as one climbed.

The struggles of the family were as formative as their joys. There were times when money was tight, and sacrifices had to be made. Thabo remembered nights when dinner was nothing more than pap and gravy, yet those were also nights filled with laughter and love, reinforcing the notion that wealth was not only measured in rands and cents, but in unbreakable family bonds.

One pivotal event in Thabo's childhood stood out as a catalyst for his ambitions. When he was ten, his family managed to scrape together enough money for a rare outing to the Apartheid Museum in Johannesburg. That visit was a revelation to young Thabo. It was not just the tales of struggle and triumph that captivated him, but the realization of the power of perseverance and belief in a cause. The stories of leaders who had risen from humble beginnings to change the course of history left an indelible mark on his young mind. He left the museum with a newfound determination to make a mark on the world, just as those heroes had.

Through his family – their values, their struggles, and their undying support – Thabo's worldview was shaped. He learned that success was multifaceted: it was about personal achievement, yes, but it was also about integrity, community, and making a difference in the lives of others.

These lessons, learned in the early years of his life, became the bedrock of his ambitions, propelling him forward on his journey to success. Within the lively and intricate community of Thabo's youth, several key figures stood out, each leaving an indelible imprint on his path towards success. These individuals were not just role models; they were the beacons that guided his understanding of what it truly meant to be successful.

1.   Gogo Zanele, the Storyteller:

Gogo Zanele, Thabo's grandmother, was a repository of wisdom and history. A retired teacher and a respected elder in the community, she had a way with stories, weaving tales from the past that captivated Thabo. Through her narratives about South Africa's history, struggles for freedom, and tales of legendary leaders, Thabo learned the importance of knowing one's roots and the power of resilience. Gogo Zanele's stories often highlighted the virtue of perseverance in the face of adversity, a lesson Thabo took to heart.

2. Mr. Khumalo, the Mentor:

Mr. Khumalo was Thabo's mathematics teacher in high school. More than just a teacher, he was a mentor who recognized Thabo's potential early on. Mr. Khumalo's teaching went beyond algebra and geometry; he taught life lessons through numbers, emphasizing logic, problem-solving, and thinking several steps ahead. He often stayed after school to help Thabo with challenging problems, not just in mathematics but in life decisions as well. Mr. Khumalo's belief in Thabo's abilities and his guidance in critical thinking were instrumental in shaping Thabo's approach to challenges and ambitions.

3. Sipho, the Entrepreneur:

Sipho was a local entrepreneur who had risen from humble beginnings to own a chain of successful spaza shops across Johannesburg. Thabo often saw him in the neighbourhood, always busy yet never too hurried to share a word of advice or encouragement. Sipho represented the kind of success Thabo aspired to – one built from the ground up through hard work and savvy. From Sipho, Thabo learned the value of self-belief and the importance of seizing opportunities. Sipho's journey taught him that success was not handed to anyone; it was earned through dedication and smart choices.

4. **Aunt Lerato, the Unsung Hero:**

Aunt Lerato, Thabo's aunt, was a nurse who worked tirelessly in the community, often going beyond her call of duty to help those in need. Her dedication to her work and the compassion she showed to every patient made a profound impact on Thabo. Aunt Lerato embodied the aspect of success that was selfless and service-oriented. Her example instilled in Thabo the understanding that true success also lay in making a positive impact on the lives of others.

Each of these figures played a pivotal role in moulding Thabo's ambitions. They collectively contributed to a multifaceted understanding of success – it was not just about achieving one's goals but doing so with integrity, perseverance, and a sense of responsibility towards others.

As Thabo grew, the lessons from these role models became the guiding principles of his journey, shaping not just his goals, but the path he chose to reach them. Thabo's journey towards ambition and success was punctuated by defining moments that shaped his path and solidified his resolve. These experiences were more than mere memories; they were the catalysts that propelled him forward, forging his character and his aspirations.

1. The Science Fair Triumph:

One of Thabo's most pivotal moments occurred during his final year at high school, at the city-wide science fair in Johannesburg. Despite his school lacking the resources of more affluent institutions, Thabo, driven by his passion for science and innovation, entered the competition with a project on renewable energy. He spent months working on it, often using makeshift materials and improvising solutions.

The day of the fair was a mix of anxiety and excitement. Thabo presented his project amidst rows of elaborate and well-funded exhibits. He felt out of place but determined. His presentation caught the attention of a panel of judges, who were impressed by his ingenuity and depth of knowledge. Thabo won second place, a victory that was not just about the accolade, but also about overcoming limitations and believing in his abilities. This triumph was a turning point for Thabo; it reinforced his belief that with creativity and determination, he could compete with the best, regardless of his background.

2. The Encounter with a Business Mogul

Another defining moment came during a chance encounter with a renowned business mogul, Mr. Mkhize. Thabo met him at a community event in Soweto, where Mr. Mkhize was a guest speaker. After the event, Thabo mustered the courage to approach him, seeking advice on pursuing success.

Expecting a brief response, Thabo was surprised when Mr. Mkhize engaged him in a lengthy conversation, sharing insights about the realities of achieving success and the importance of resilience and ethics.

Mr. Mkhize's words struck a chord with Thabo, especially his emphasis on the balance between ambition and moral integrity. This encounter left a lasting impression on Thabo, shaping his perception of success as a journey that requires not just hard work and talent, but also a strong ethical compass and a commitment to one's values. In the heart of Johannesburg, amidst the hustle and daily rhythm of the city, Thabo's dreams and aspirations took shape, reflecting a vision of success that was both personal and expansive. His ambitions, though grounded in the reality of his upbringing, reached beyond the skies of his beloved city.

3. The Vision of Technological Innovation:

At this stage in his life, Thabo's primary dream was to become a pioneer in the field of technology and innovation in South Africa. Inspired by the global tech revolution and determined to bring such advancements to his homeland, he envisioned creating a technology start-up that would not only be successful but also transformative. He dreamed of developing technological solutions that addressed local challenges, such as renewable energy, efficient farming techniques, and accessible healthcare technology.

For Thabo, success in this realm meant making a significant impact on the lives of ordinary South Africans, improving their quality of life through innovation.

4. Building a Community Legacy:

Thabo's aspirations were not confined to personal achievements in technology. He also dreamed of giving back to his community in Soweto and beyond. He envisioned establishing a foundation that would support education and entrepreneurship for young South Africans, especially those from underprivileged backgrounds. By providing scholarships, mentorship programs, and seed funding for start-ups, Thabo aimed to cultivate a new generation of innovators and leaders. His idea of success included creating a lasting legacy that would uplift and empower others.

5. The Path to Achievement:

Achieving these dreams was not a vague notion for Thabo. He had a clear plan of action, which involved pursuing higher education in the field of computer science and business. He was determined to gain the knowledge and skills necessary to bring his technological aspirations to fruition. Thabo also understood the importance of networking and sought to connect with like-minded individuals and potential mentors in the tech industry. He believed in the power of collaboration and community in realizing big dreams.

6. Upholding Values and Integrity:

Amidst his ambitions, Thabo remained committed to maintaining his integrity and staying true to his values. He knew the path to success was often riddled with ethical dilemmas and temptations to take shortcuts. However, Thabo was resolute in achieving his goals honourably, without compromising the values instilled in him by his family and community. Thabo's dreams and aspirations set the stage for a journey filled with ambition, innovation, and a deep sense of social responsibility. His goals were not just a ladder to personal success but a bridge towards creating a broader impact. This vision of success was a driving force for Thabo, propelling him forward in a journey that promised challenges, learning, and growth.

In the midst of Thabo's dreams and the vibrant energy of Johannesburg, subtle undercurrents hinted at the challenges and obstacles that lay ahead in his path to success. These foreshadows, woven into the fabric of his daily life and the city around him, served as a sobering reminder that the road to achievement would be anything but straightforward.

1. Societal Pressures and Expectations:

As Thabo shared his aspirations with others, he often encountered a mix of reactions. While many expressed admiration and support, there were also those who voiced scepticism and doubt. These interactions hinted at societal pressures and expectations that Thabo would have to navigate. In a community where traditional paths were often favoured, venturing into the uncertain world of technology and entrepreneurship was viewed with apprehension. Thabo would need to muster not just determination but also the courage to defy conventional expectations and chart his own course.

2. Economic and Resource Constraints:

Thabo was acutely aware of the economic challenges that lay ahead. Johannesburg, despite its bustling economy, was also a city of disparities. Access to capital, resources, and opportunities in the tech sector was not evenly distributed. Thabo knew that turning his dreams into reality would require overcoming significant financial hurdles, finding investors who believed in his vision, and creatively maximizing limited resources.

3. Navigating the Competitive Tech Landscape:

The technology sector in South Africa, and particularly in Johannesburg, was rapidly evolving and highly competitive. Thabo understood that breaking into this industry would be a formidable task. He would need to stay ahead of emerging trends, continually innovate, and distinguish himself in a crowded field. This competitive landscape foreshadowed a relentless pursuit of excellence and the need for continuous learning and adaptation.

4. Balancing Personal Ambitions with Community Values:

Thabo's ambitions, while noble, also posed an internal conflict. He deeply valued his community and the principles he had grown up with, yet he also recognized that achieving his goals might require stepping into worlds far removed from his familiar surroundings. This tension foreshadowed a balancing act between personal aspirations and staying true to his roots and values.

5.   The Unpredictability of Johannesburg's Pulse:

Finally, Johannesburg itself presented a backdrop of uncertainty and change. The city's dynamic nature, while a source of inspiration, also meant that Thabo would need to be prepared for unforeseen changes in the social, economic, and political landscape. The city's pulse was unpredictable, and its challenges were as diverse as its opportunities.

As the Johannesburg sun dipped below the horizon, painting the sky in hues of orange and purple, Thabo stood at the balcony of his family home in Soweto, gazing out at the sprawling city lights. It was a view he had seen countless times, yet tonight, it held a different meaning. Tonight, it was not just a cityscape; it was a canvas of possibilities, a map of his future journey.

In his hand, he held a letter, its contents both an invitation and a challenge. It was an acceptance letter from one of South Africa's most prestigious universities, offering him a place in their esteemed computer science program. This was the opportunity he had been working towards, the first significant step on the path to realizing his dreams.

Yet, as he stood there, a mix of excitement and apprehension swirling within him, Thabo knew that accepting this opportunity meant stepping into a world vastly different from the one he knew. It meant leaving the comfort and familiarity of his community, venturing into uncharted territories, and facing challenges on a scale he had never experienced before.

The decision weighed heavily on him. On one hand, there was the safety of the known, the warmth of his family, and the camaraderie of his community. On the other, there was the allure of the unknown, the promise of growth, and the pursuit of his ambitions.

As the night deepened, Thabo's thoughts turned to the influential figures in his life – Gogo Zanele's stories of resilience, Mr. Khumalo's lessons in critical thinking, Sipho's entrepreneurial spirit, and Aunt Lerato's selfless service. Each had, in their own way, prepared him for this moment.

Taking a deep breath, Thabo felt a resolve solidifying within him. He knew that to achieve the greatness he envisioned, he would have to embrace this change, step out of his comfort zone, and confront the challenges head-on. This was his moment to leap, to soar beyond the confines of Soweto and make his mark in the broader tapestry of Johannesburg and beyond.

As he turned from the balcony, letter in hand, Thabo was no longer just a dreamer; he was a dreamer in motion. The journey ahead would test him, shape him, and require all the courage, intelligence, and determination he possessed. But he was ready. Ready to turn his dreams into reality, ready to face the world, ready to step into the next chapter of his life. The city of Johannesburg, with all its complexities and opportunities, awaited him.

CROSSING PATHS IN PRETORIA

As the early morning sun cast a golden hue over the Jacaranda-lined streets, Thabo stepped off the bus into Pretoria. The air here was different – it held a quiet promise, a stark contrast to the relentless pulse of Johannesburg. Thabo took a moment to absorb his surroundings, the city's calm enveloping him like a gentle embrace. This was a new chapter, a new city, a new beginning.

Pretoria, known as the administrative capital, presented a world apart from the constant motion and buzz of Johannesburg. The streets were less crowded, the buildings bore the weight of history, and there was a sense of order and purpose in the air. Thabo was struck by the abundance of green spaces – parks filled with sprawling lawns and the famous Jacarandas that turned the city into a sea of purple each spring.

As he walked through the city, Thabo noticed the grandeur of the Union Buildings, the seat of the South African government, perched majestically on Meintjieskop. Its architectural splendour and historical significance reminded him of the country's journey to democracy, a narrative that resonated deeply with his own aspirations. The pace of life in Pretoria was noticeably more relaxed than in Johannesburg. People seemed to move with a sense of certainty and calm, a rhythm that was new to Thabo. He relished the change, feeling it provided a fresh perspective, a different kind of canvas for his ambitions.

Yet, beneath the city's serene exterior, Thabo sensed an undercurrent of energy and potential. Pretoria was not just a city of bureaucrats and diplomats; it was also a hub of education and innovation. The university campus, a blend of modern and old architecture, buzzed with the aspirations of students from diverse backgrounds. Here, in these halls of learning, new ideas and innovations were taking shape, and Thabo felt a surge of excitement at being part of this vibrant academic community.

But with this excitement came a twinge of nervousness. Thabo was stepping into uncharted territory. He was no longer just a dreamer from Soweto; he was now a young man in a new city, about to embark on a journey that would test his resolve and shape his future. As Thabo settled into his new surroundings, he felt a growing conviction that Pretoria would be the forge in which his dreams and ambitions would be tempered and transformed. This city, with its unique blend of history, tranquillity, and intellectual fervour, was the perfect backdrop for the next phase of his journey.

In Pretoria, Thabo was not just starting a new academic chapter; he was stepping onto a larger stage, one that promised to bring him closer to his dreams of innovation and success. As Thabo embarked on his university journey in Pretoria, the initial weeks were a whirlwind of adjustment and adaptation. The academic rigor at the university was a notch higher than he had anticipated. Lectures were dense with information, and the expectations from professors were daunting.

Thabo found himself grappling with complex theories and concepts, a far cry from the more straightforward learning he was accustomed to in Johannesburg.

The diversity of the student body was both fascinating and challenging for Thabo. He met peers from various parts of South Africa, each bringing their unique perspectives and experiences. Conversations ranged from intense political debates to cultural exchanges, exposing Thabo to a myriad of viewpoints. While this diversity enriched his learning, it also required him to navigate and understand the complexities of a multi-cultural environment.

Despite these challenges, Thabo was determined to thrive. He spent long hours in the library, poring over textbooks and academic journals, gradually finding his footing in the demanding academic landscape. He also learned to engage in discussions, listening attentively and contributing thoughtfully, valuing the richness that diverse opinions brought to his education.

Off-campus, Thabo found a modest room in a shared house close to the university. The place was small but had a certain charm, with a window that overlooked a quiet street lined with blooming Jacarandas. This room became his refuge, a place where he could reflect, study, and rest away from the bustling campus life.

His housemates were a mix of local and international students, each with their own stories and dreams. They introduced Thabo to the social and cultural life of Pretoria. From braais in the backyard to exploring local markets and cafes, Thabo began to feel a sense of belonging in this new city. His housemates, each with their unique way of navigating university life, offered insights and advice that helped Thabo adjust to his new environment.

Weekends were a time to explore Pretoria, from its museums and historical sites to the vibrant street markets and cafes. Thabo found himself enamoured with the city's blend of history, culture, and modernity. The relaxed pace of Pretoria provided a welcome respite from the intensity of university life. As Thabo settled into this new phase of his life, he began to embrace the challenges and opportunities it presented.

University life was shaping him not just academically but also personally, broadening his perspectives and deepening his understanding of the world around him. In Pretoria, amidst the academic challenges and the new cultural experiences, Thabo was laying the groundwork for his future aspirations. In the dynamic and intellectually charged atmosphere of the university, Thabo's encounters with two exceptional individuals would significantly shape his path and perspective.

Professor Ndebele: The Demanding Mentor

Thabo first met Professor Ndebele in an advanced computer science class. Known for his ground-breaking research in artificial intelligence, Professor Ndebele was a towering figure in the academic community, both revered and feared for his exacting standards. From the first lecture, Thabo was struck by the professor's deep knowledge and passion for computer science. His teaching style was rigorous and demanding, pushing students to not just understand but to innovate and think critically.

Thabo found himself simultaneously intimidated and inspired by Professor Ndebele. The professor's assignments were challenging, often requiring late nights of coding and problem-solving. Yet, it was under this pressure that Thabo's skills and understanding of computer science began to flourish. Professor Ndebele took notice of Thabo's dedication and potential, offering guidance and pushing him to delve deeper into complex topics.

In Professor Ndebele, Thabo found a mentor who challenged him to reach beyond his comfort zone. The professor's insistence on excellence and his ability to inspire innovative thinking left a profound impact on Thabo, shaping his approach to his studies and his future ambitions in technology.

Dr. Mokoena: The Entrepreneurial Guide

Another pivotal encounter for Thabo was with Dr. Mokoena, a guest lecturer and a successful entrepreneur in the tech industry. Dr. Mokoena's lecture on technology entrepreneurship was a revelation for Thabo. Here was someone who had translated academic knowledge into real-world impact, embodying the type of success Thabo aspired to achieve.

After the lecture, Thabo approached Dr. Mokoena, and the two struck up a conversation that marked the beginning of an invaluable mentorship. Dr. Mokoena, with his practical experience and insightful views on the tech industry, provided a different perspective from the academic rigor of university. He spoke candidly about the challenges of starting a tech business, the importance of resilience, and the need to constantly adapt and innovate.

Over time, Dr. Mokoena became an informal mentor to Thabo, offering advice, sharing experiences, and sometimes providing a sounding board for Thabo's burgeoning business ideas. His journey as an entrepreneur and his approach to overcoming obstacles and seizing opportunities deeply influenced Thabo's aspirations and understanding of what it took to succeed in the competitive world of technology.

These encounters with mentors – one in the academic realm and the other from the industry – provided Thabo with a rich, multifaceted understanding of his field. Professor Ndebele and Dr. Mokoena, in their unique ways, contributed significantly to Thabo's growth, equipping him with the knowledge, skills, and mindset necessary to navigate the complexities of the tech world and to forge his own path to success.

Thabo's journey at the university was not just about academic and professional growth; it was also a time for forming significant relationships that would shape his understanding of rivalry, friendship, and collaboration. One of Thabo's most notable encounters was with Lindiwe, a fellow computer science student whose ambition and talent matched his own. Lindiwe, with her sharp intellect and assertive nature, quickly made a name for herself in class. Initially, Thabo viewed her as a rival, someone who challenged his position as one of the top students. Their early interactions were marked by competitive debates and a mutual desire to outdo each other in assignments and projects.

However, as they worked together on a group project, their rivalry began to evolve into a deeper understanding and respect. Thabo admired Lindiwe's analytical skills and her ability to approach problems from unique perspectives. Lindiwe, in turn, respected Thabo's dedication and technical prowess.

This mutual admiration slowly transformed their rivalry into a supportive friendship. They began to collaborate more, learning from each other and pushing each other to excel. Their competitive spirit remained, but it was now coupled with a sense of camaraderie and shared goals. Another significant relationship Thabo formed was with Sizwe, a well-connected and charismatic student in the business school. Sizwe, known for his extensive network and social skills, introduced Thabo to various student organizations and professional circles.

Through Sizwe, Thabo attended events and meetups that broadened his horizons and connected him with influential figures in the tech industry. However, Thabo soon began to notice certain facets of Sizwe's personality that gave him pause. While Sizwe was undeniably helpful and friendly, there was an undercurrent of competitiveness and a tendency to use relationships for personal gain. Thabo observed how Sizwe would often change his opinions and attitudes to fit the crowd, revealing a certain duplicity in his character.

This realization made Thabo cautious in his interactions with Sizwe. He appreciated the doors that Sizwe's network opened for him but remained wary of becoming too reliant on Sizwe's influence. Thabo understood that in the realm of networking and relationships, it was important to discern genuine intentions and maintain one's integrity.

As Thabo delved deeper into his university journey, he found himself navigating a complex web of academic and social challenges, each demanding a different facet of his resilience and adaptability. The academic demands at the university were relentless. Thabo's coursework in computer science was both fascinating and overwhelming, with a steady stream of assignments, projects, and exams. He spent long hours in the library, often staying up late to master difficult concepts or work on coding projects. The pressure to maintain his grades and understand complex material was immense.

Amidst this academic rigor, Thabo occasionally battled moments of self-doubt. He questioned his abilities and his place in the competitive university environment, especially when he compared himself to his peers. These moments of uncertainty were challenging, but Thabo found strength in his goals and ambitions. Remembering his dreams of innovation and impact, he pushed through the doubts, using them as fuel to work harder and stay focused.

Balancing his rigorous study schedule with social activities was another challenge Thabo faced. University life was not just about academics; it was also a time for personal growth and making connections. Thabo wanted to experience the full spectrum of university life, from attending cultural events and social gatherings to participating in student organizations.

He learned to manage his time effectively, setting aside dedicated hours for studying and allowing himself to enjoy social events and relax. This balance was crucial in maintaining his mental and emotional well-being. The social interactions and leisure activities provided a much-needed respite from academic pressures and a chance to build friendships and create memories.

Recognizing the importance of practical experience and networking, Thabo began to participate in tech meetups and seminars in Pretoria. These events were gateways into the burgeoning tech scene of the city, offering insights into the latest industry trends and opportunities to meet professionals and entrepreneurs. Attending these events, Thabo immersed himself in the world of technology beyond the university. He engaged in discussions about emerging technologies, attended workshops on various tech topics, and even volunteered at some events. This exposure was invaluable in broadening his understanding of the tech industry and in forming connections that could be pivotal for his future career.

Thabo's navigation of academic and social challenges at the university was a delicate balancing act, one that involved managing pressures, overcoming self-doubt, and seizing opportunities for growth and networking. These experiences were integral in shaping him into a well-rounded individual, ready to face the complexities of the real world.

Thabo's journey through university life in Pretoria was not just an academic pursuit but a profound learning and growing experience, shaping his understanding of the subtleties of human relationships and the realities of thriving in a competitive environment.

As Thabo delved deeper into his university life, he became acutely aware of the complexities inherent in relationships within a competitive academic setting. He observed how ambition could both forge alliances and fuel rivalries. Interactions with peers like Lindiwe and Sizwe taught him the nuances of navigating these dynamics. Thabo learned to balance healthy competition with collaboration, understanding that success in such an environment required more than just individual brilliance; it required the ability to work effectively with others.

Diplomacy became a key skill for Thabo. He honed his ability to communicate effectively, to negotiate and resolve conflicts, and to build relationships based on mutual respect and shared goals. This was particularly evident in group projects and discussions, where he learned to listen, contribute thoughtfully, and sometimes compromise to achieve the best outcomes. Another crucial lesson for Thabo was the importance of networking.

Through his interactions at university events, tech meetups, and seminars, he realized that building a network was not just about collecting contacts but about forming meaningful connections. He learned to engage with others genuinely, to offer and seek help, and to establish relationships that could provide support, advice, and opportunities in the future. Thabo also understood that networking was a two-way street. He made efforts to be a valuable connection himself, sharing knowledge, offering assistance, and staying in touch with the contacts he made. This approach helped him build a robust network that would be invaluable in his professional journey.

Thabo's experiences at university also began to shape his views on leadership and collaboration. He took on leadership roles in student projects and organizations, which taught him about responsibility, team management, and decision-making. These experiences highlighted the importance of leading by example, motivating team members, and fostering a collaborative environment.

Working on diverse teams, Thabo learned the value of different perspectives and skill sets. He saw first-hand how collaborative efforts often led to more innovative and effective solutions than working in isolation. These experiences reinforced his belief in the power of teamwork and collective effort, especially in a field as dynamic and multifaceted as technology.

Finally, Thabo's time in Pretoria gave him a realistic understanding of the competitive nature of the tech field. He learned that success in this industry required not just technical skills but also adaptability, continuous learning, and the ability to stay ahead of trends.

These realizations were crucial in preparing Thabo for the challenges of the professional world. Thabo's growth during his university years was comprehensive. He emerged not just with academic knowledge but with vital life skills—diplomacy, networking, leadership, and collaboration—that would be instrumental in his future endeavours. His experiences in Pretoria shaped him into a well-rounded individual, ready to navigate the complexities of the competitive world of technology.

As the chapter draws to a close, a pivotal moment arrives in Thabo's life, one that could potentially alter the trajectory of his journey. It was during a routine visit to Dr. Mokoena's office to discuss a class project when the unexpected opportunity was presented. Dr. Mokoena, having observed Thabo's passion and proficiency in technology, offered him a chance to work on a cutting-edge project in the field of artificial intelligence, a project that promised to be at the forefront of technological innovation in South Africa.

This opportunity was what Thabo had always dreamed of: to be involved in work that was not only challenging and ground-breaking but also had the potential to make a significant impact. The project, however, was not without its risks. It was an ambitious venture, requiring a level of commitment and expertise that went beyond what Thabo had experienced in his academic pursuits.

It meant working alongside seasoned professionals and potentially putting his academic work on hold. As Thabo sat in Dr. Mokoena's office, the weight of the decision pressed heavily upon him. On one hand, this was a once-in-a-lifetime opportunity to dive into real-world applications of his studies, to contribute to something that could shape the future of technology in his country. It was a chance to grow, to test his abilities, and to make his mark in the tech world.

On the other hand, the project presented significant uncertainties. It was a venture into uncharted territory, stepping out of the familiar structure and security of university life. The risk of failure was real, and the thought of veering off his academic path was daunting. There were also practical considerations – balancing project work with his studies, the possibility of delaying his graduation, and the impact on his carefully laid plans.

The chapter ends with Thabo looking out of Dr. Mokoena's office window, contemplating the Johannesburg skyline in the distance. He is at a crossroads, torn between the safe path of continuing his academic journey as planned and the risky but potentially rewarding path of venturing into the professional world. This decision was more than just a choice about a project; it was a decision about the kind of future he wanted to carve for himself.

As Thabo pondered his options, he realized that this decision was a defining moment in his journey. It was an opportunity to step out of his comfort zone and embrace the challenges of the real world. The chapter closes with Thabo deep in thought, recognizing that whichever path he chose, it would mark the beginning of a new chapter in his life, a chapter filled with unknowns but brimming with possibilities.

This conclusion sets a tone of anticipation and introspection, leaving the reader eager to learn about Thabo's decision and how it will shape his journey ahead. The opportunity presented to him symbolizes the transition from theory to practice, from learning to doing, and the challenges and rewards that come with taking risks.

TRIUMPHS AND TRIALS

As Thabo stepped into the realm of the cutting-edge technology project under Dr. Mokoena's guidance, he entered a world where innovation and rapid development were the norms. The project, cantered on developing advanced artificial intelligence solutions for real-world applications, was both daunting and thrilling.

In the initial weeks, Thabo's transition from academic theory to practical application was a steep learning curve. He immersed himself in the latest AI research, spent hours coding and testing, and participated in brainstorming sessions that stretched late into the evenings. The pace was intense, but Thabo thrived in this environment, his passion for technology fuelling his dedication.

His innovative approach and fresh perspective soon began to bear fruit. Thabo introduced a novel algorithm that significantly improved the efficiency of the project's data processing. This contribution was a breakthrough for the team, and it didn't go unnoticed. His colleagues, some of whom were seasoned professionals in the field, began to look at him not just as a young newcomer but as a valuable member of the team.

Thabo's early achievements also brought recognition from Dr. Mokoena, who commended him for his ingenuity and hard work. This acknowledgment was particularly gratifying for Thabo, reinforcing his belief in his decision to join the project and pursue his passion.

These initial successes in the project were pivotal for Thabo. They were not merely professional accomplishments; they represented his transition from a student to a burgeoning professional in the tech industry. Each achievement bolstered his confidence and solidified his commitment to the project and his future career.

This phase of Thabo's journey was marked by a sense of accomplishment and a realization of his potential. The challenges and learning opportunities that came with the project were shaping him into a skilled and innovative technologist. As he continued to contribute and grow within the project, Thabo's early successes laid a strong foundation for his emerging career in technology.

The exhilaration of early triumphs in the technology project soon gave way to the reality of its formidable challenges. Thabo found himself at the deep end of advanced artificial intelligence work, an area brimming with complexities and incessant demands for innovation.

The technical aspects of the project were particularly demanding. Thabo was tasked with developing algorithms that were at the cutting edge of AI technology. This endeavour required a deep understanding of complex concepts and the application of advanced data analysis techniques. The algorithms he worked on were crucial to the success of the project, and the pressure to get them right was immense.

To add to the challenge, Thabo needed to quickly familiarize himself with new programming languages and software tools. This learning process was intense and time-consuming, often requiring him to spend extra hours self-studying and practicing. The pace of learning was like nothing he had experienced in his academic life, pushing him to expand his technical abilities and adapt quickly to new information and techniques.

Along with the technical challenges, Thabo grappled with the pressure of delivering results. The project was high-stakes, and the team relied on each contribution to move forward. The fear of underperforming or causing delays was a constant presence in Thabo's mind. He was acutely aware that his performance could not only impact the project but also his future career prospects in the technology field.

Despite these daunting challenges, Thabo did not waver. He approached each hurdle with a mindset that saw obstacles as opportunities for growth. His perseverance was fuelled by his passion for technology and his desire to make a meaningful contribution to the field.

Thabo spent long nights troubleshooting code, experimenting with different approaches, and seeking feedback from more experienced colleagues. He took advantage of every learning opportunity, attending workshops and seminars to enhance his skills. Gradually, his efforts began to pay off. Thabo's solutions became more refined, and his input more valuable to the project.

Each challenge surmounted added to Thabo's experience and confidence. He was not only honing his technical skills but also learning vital lessons in resilience, problem-solving, and working under pressure. These experiences were shaping him into a more competent and confident technologist.

As Thabo's expertise and contributions to the technology project grew, so too did his visibility within the team. With this increased recognition, however, came an unforeseen and unsettling challenge: the undercurrents of envy from some of his peers.

Initially, the signs were subtle and easy to overlook. Thabo noticed occasional offhand remarks that didn't quite sound like genuine praise. For instance, after successfully troubleshooting a complex problem, a colleague remarked, "You're lucky to always guess right," a comment that seemed to attribute Thabo's success to luck rather than skill. There were backhanded compliments too, where his abilities were acknowledged but with an undertone that seemed to diminish his hard work.

The hidden envy became more pronounced in team meetings. Thabo observed that some of his suggestions, which were once welcomed, now faced undue scrutiny. A few team members began to question his methods and the viability of his ideas, often without substantial reasoning. This shift was subtle but consistent, creating an undercurrent of tension that Thabo found hard to ignore.

These interactions were a stark contrast to the straightforward competitiveness he had experienced in the academic setting. In university, rivals challenged each other openly, but in this professional environment, the rivalry was cloaked in collegiality, making it more complex and difficult to navigate.

Thabo was initially taken aback by this change in dynamics. He had expected technical challenges in the project but was unprepared for the interpersonal ones. He realized that professional success was not just about one's technical abilities but also about navigating the intricate human elements of the workplace. Understanding and managing relationships, deciphering underlying motives, and maintaining a positive and professional demeanour were skills just as essential as technical expertise.

This realization was a pivotal moment in Thabo's professional development. He began to approach his interactions with colleagues more cautiously, striving to maintain a balance between assertiveness and diplomacy. Thabo also sought advice from mentors like Dr. Mokoena, who provided insights on handling workplace envy and the importance of staying focused on one's goals.

Despite these challenges, Thabo's resolve to succeed and contribute meaningfully to the project remained unshaken. He continued to focus on his work, choosing to let his results speak for themselves. He also worked on strengthening his alliances within the team, building relationships based on mutual respect and collaboration.

As Thabo navigated the complex dynamics of the workplace, marked by hidden envy and subtle rivalries, he found himself at a crossroads of personal and professional development. This period of introspection and challenge became a crucible for his growth, forging resilience and a deeper understanding of the realities of professional life.

In moments of quiet reflection, Thabo revisited the experiences he had encountered since joining the tech project. He thought about the technical hurdles he had overcome, the recognition he had earned, and the undercurrents of envy he now faced. These reflections brought clarity to Thabo about the multifaceted nature of a professional career. He understood that success was not just about achieving technical excellence but also about dealing with complex human emotions and relationships.

Thabo recalled the advice and lessons from his mentors, particularly from Dr. Mokoena, who had once spoken about the inevitability of encountering envy and opposition in any path that leads to success. These lessons emphasized the importance of resilience, the ability to stay focused on one's goals, and the need to uphold one's values and integrity in the face of challenges.

Empowered by these reflections, Thabo made a conscious decision not to let the negative attitudes of others derail him. He recognized that allowing the envy of others to impact his work would only hinder his progress. Instead, he chose to channel his energies into his contributions to the project, maintaining a positive and professional attitude.

Thabo's approach to his work became more focused and determined. He continued to put forth innovative ideas, collaborate effectively with his team, and contribute to the project's advancements. His commitment to the project and his unflagging spirit in the face of adversity did not go unnoticed. It earned him not only respect from many of his colleagues but also reinforced his reputation as a valuable and reliable member of the team.

This period of reflection and resilience was transformative for Thabo. It strengthened his character, enhanced his professional capabilities, and deepened his understanding of the complexities of working within a team. Thabo emerged from this experience with a newfound resilience and a clearer vision of the type of professional and individual he aspired to be. As the chapter "Triumphs and Trials" draws to a close, it culminates in a moment of triumph for Thabo, marking a significant milestone in both the project and his personal journey.

After months of relentless work, overcoming technical challenges, and navigating complex team dynamics, Thabo's efforts culminated in a significant breakthrough. He developed an innovative solution that enhanced the project's AI algorithm, drastically improving its efficiency and accuracy. This breakthrough was a critical turning point for the project, propelling it forward and bringing it closer to its ambitious goals.

Thabo's achievement did not go unnoticed. Dr. Mokoena, along with the rest of the team, recognized and celebrated his contribution. Receiving accolades from Dr. Mokoena, someone he deeply respected and admired, was particularly gratifying for Thabo.

It was an affirmation of his skills, his hard work, and his potential as a technologist. This recognition also served to cement his standing within the team, showcasing his ability to contribute significantly to high-stakes, innovative work.

This pivotal achievement was more than just a professional victory for Thabo; it was a moment that reinforced his confidence in his chosen path. It validated his decision to step out of his academic comfort zone and take on the challenges of the real world. The experience bolstered his belief in his capabilities and in the importance of perseverance and resilience in the face of adversity.

As the chapter ends, Thabo reflects on his journey thus far – from the initial excitement of joining the project to the challenges he faced and the growth he experienced. This reflection is filled with a sense of accomplishment and a deeper understanding of his own strengths and potential. Thabo realizes that this achievement is not just a milestone in the project but also a crucial step in his own personal and professional development.

With this achievement, Thabo looks towards the future with renewed vigour and optimism. He is more determined than ever to continue his journey in technology, driven by the knowledge that his contributions can lead to meaningful advancements and impact. The chapter closes with Thabo poised to continue his journey, equipped with newfound experiences, skills, and a stronger sense of purpose.

The evening of the Masked Ball, a prestigious event in Johannesburg's social calendar, was one Thabo would not soon forget. As he stepped into the venue, a magnificent ballroom in one of the city's most luxurious hotels, he was immediately enveloped in an atmosphere of opulence and splendour.

The ballroom was a vision of elegance, adorned with crystal chandeliers that cast a soft, golden light over the guests. The walls were lined with intricate tapestries and the floors with polished marble, reflecting the shimmering lights and the vibrant colours of the attendees' masks and gowns. Tables were set with fine China and sparkling glassware, and the air resonated with the soft melodies of a string quartet playing in the background.

Guests moved through the room like characters from a grandiose play, their faces partially concealed behind masks of feathers, jewels, and intricate designs. The masks added a layer of intrigue and mystique to the event, allowing the city's elite to mingle with a sense of anonymity and freedom. The attire was equally extravagant, with women in flowing gowns and men in sharp tuxedos, each adding to the allure and elegance of the evening.

The air was filled with a mix of expensive perfumes and the subtle aroma of gourmet dishes being served. Waiters glided through the crowd, offering trays of exquisite canapés and flutes of champagne. The murmur of conversation was a blend of laughter, business talk, and the clinking of glasses, creating a buzz that was both exhilarating and overwhelming.

For Thabo, this event was a far cry from his usual environment. He was accustomed to the more straightforward settings of tech meetups and university halls. Here, amidst Johannesburg's most influential and successful personalities, he found himself in a world that was both alien and fascinating. It was a world that spoke of power, success, and the finer things in life – elements that were becoming increasingly relevant in his own journey.

The Masked Ball was more than just a social event; it was a symbol of the heights Thabo aspired to reach. It represented a fusion of his past and future – a reminder of where he came from and a glimpse of the world he was stepping into. As he mingled with the guests, Thabo felt a mix of awe and determination. The grandeur of the ball reinforced his aspirations, motivating him to continue his pursuit of success in the tech world.

The Masked Ball presented Thabo with an unparalleled opportunity to mingle with Johannesburg's crème de la crème, a gathering of individuals whose success stories were as diverse as they were inspiring. As he navigated through the sea of masked faces, Thabo found himself in a world far removed from the academic and technological realms he was accustomed to.

Thabo's interactions varied widely throughout the evening. He found himself conversing with a tech mogul who had pioneered some of the most innovative software in the industry, their discussion delving into the future of technology and its impact on society. In another encounter, he met a renowned business leader whose empire spanned across continents, offering Thabo insights into the world of global commerce and the intricacies of managing vast enterprises.

The ball also brought Thabo into contact with personalities from the arts and philanthropy. He was captivated by the stories of a celebrated artist whose paintings reflected the vibrant culture and history of South Africa. A philanthropist shared her journey of establishing foundations that supported education and healthcare initiatives across the country, igniting in Thabo a deep sense of admiration and a rekindled interest in societal impact.

These interactions gave Thabo a glimpse into the lives of those who had achieved remarkable success in their respective fields. He heard tales of challenges overcome, risks taken, and the relentless pursuit of goals. The conversations often revolved around achievements and accolades, but they also revealed the sacrifices and responsibilities that came with such success.

For Thabo, every conversation was a learning experience. He listened intently, asked questions, and absorbed the wisdom and advice shared by these accomplished individuals. Their stories were not just narratives of triumph but also lessons in resilience, innovation, and the importance of giving back to the community.

Amidst these exchanges, Thabo found himself reflecting on his journey. He realized how far he had come and how much further he aspired to go. The elite of Johannesburg, with their diverse accomplishments and experiences, represented the myriad paths that success could take. For Thabo, this was both an eye-opener and a motivator, a confirmation that his ambitions were valid and achievable.

As the section concludes, Thabo steps away from the crowd for a moment, taking in the atmosphere and pondering the conversations he had. The ball was more than a social event; it was a convergence of inspiration and aspiration. Thabo felt his horizons broadening, his aspirations evolving not just in scale but also in depth. The evening had cemented his determination to carve out his own path of success, one that would hopefully see him return to such gatherings not just as a guest but as a celebrated contributor.

As the evening progressed at the Masked Ball, Thabo's initial awe and admiration for the glittering world of Johannesburg's elite began to mingle with a more nuanced understanding. The more he observed and listened, the more he became aware of the subtle complexities underlying the glamorous façade of success.

Thabo noticed that many of the compliments exchanged among the guests carried an undercurrent of comparison and competition. Praises, while outwardly gracious, often came with a subtle one-upmanship. A congratulatory remark on a business deal, for example, would be followed by a mention of another, seemingly more impressive deal. These exchanges, while polite and sophisticated in their delivery, revealed a constant jostling for status and recognition.

As he mingled, Thabo overheard snippets of conversations that unveiled the more envious side of success. Remarks about the rapid rise of a new entrepreneur, the sudden acclaim of an artist, or the unexpected success of a tech start-up were often laced with thinly veiled jealousy. It was as if the achievements of one were seen as a challenge to the status of others.

This duality of success – the intertwining of admiration with envy – was a revelation to Thabo. He began to see that the journey to the top was fraught not just with external challenges but also with the complex dynamics of human emotions. Success, he realized, was not just a path to admiration and respect but also one that could attract envy and rivalry.

Witnessing these dynamics made Thabo reflect on his journey and the path he was on. He understood that if he were to achieve the success he aspired to, he too might become the subject of such dual sentiments. This realization was sobering, yet it also steeled his resolve. He recognized that navigating the landscape of success would require not just professional skills but also emotional intelligence and a thick skin.

The evening at the Masked Ball thus became a turning point in Thabo's understanding of what it meant to be successful. He saw that success was a multifaceted entity, accompanied by both light and shadow. The experience at the ball illuminated the reality that true success would involve not just reaching his goals but also managing the complex web of relationships and perceptions that came with it.

As Thabo left the ball that night, he carried with him not just the glitz and glamour of the evening but also a deeper insight into the nature of success.

He resolved that in his pursuit of success, he would strive to maintain his integrity, be mindful of the feelings of others, and be prepared for the range of reactions his achievements might evoke. In the midst of the Masked Ball's opulence, Thabo experienced a moment of profound realization that significantly altered his perception of success and its repercussions.

As he moved through the crowd, Thabo accidentally became an unseen listener to a conversation about himself. A group of guests, unaware of his presence nearby, were discussing his recent contributions to the high-profile tech project. The tones of their voices varied – some spoke with genuine admiration about the innovation and impact of his work, while others carried a hint of scepticism and envy. "He's risen quickly, hasn't he? Almost too quickly for someone so young," one guest remarked, subtly questioning the legitimacy of Thabo's achievements.

This moment was a revelation for Thabo. Until now, he had viewed success predominantly as a source of pride and recognition. However, overhearing this conversation unveiled a different aspect – the envy and judgment that often accompany success. It became clear that achievements could be perceived through various lenses, not all of them positive.

Thabo's experience at the ball, particularly this overheard conversation, metaphorically paralleled the physical masks worn by the guests. Just as the masks concealed the wearers' identities, so too did they hide the complex mix of emotions – admiration, envy, scepticism – that success in any field could evoke. Thabo realized that in the journey toward success, one often encounters hidden sentiments that are not immediately apparent.

This incident prompted Thabo to reflect on how he would handle success and its accompanying challenges. He understood that with recognition would come scrutiny and not all of it would be favourable. This understanding was pivotal in preparing him to navigate the multifaceted nature of his career path and personal growth.

As Thabo left the conversation and moved back into the crowd, he did so with a more balanced view of success. He recognized that while achievements bring joy and satisfaction, they also require one to be prepared for less favourable reactions. This realization was not disheartening for Thabo; rather, it equipped him with a more realistic perspective on the journey ahead. It underscored the importance of staying grounded and true to oneself, regardless of external perceptions.

As the Masked Ball wound down, the laughter and music fading into a soft echo, Thabo retreated to a quieter part of the venue, finding solace in a secluded corner. Here, amidst the waning clamour of the event, he engaged in a moment of introspection, reflecting on the evening's revelations and their implications for his journey. The ball had been an eye-opener for Thabo, illuminating the multifaceted nature of success.

He pondered over the conversations he had heard and participated in, the subtle undercurrents of envy and admiration, and the realization that success was not a straightforward path to glory. It was, instead, a complex journey filled with varied reactions and perceptions.

Thabo recognized that to navigate this landscape effectively, he would need more than just technical expertise and professional acumen. He would also require a high degree of emotional intelligence – the ability to understand and manage his emotions and those of others. This skill would be crucial in dealing with the myriad of responses his successes and failures might elicit.

Amidst these reflections, Thabo understood the importance of maintaining a strong sense of self. He realized that his identity and values should not be swayed by the opinions and perceptions of others. Whether faced with praise or criticism, he needed to remain grounded in who he was and what he stood for. This resolve to stay true to himself was reinforced by the evening's experiences.

Thabo reaffirmed his commitment to his goals. He reminded himself of why he embarked on this path – to innovate, to contribute to the field of technology, and to make a meaningful impact. The recognition that success comes with its share of challenges only strengthened his determination to pursue his aspirations with integrity and purpose. As

Thabo stepped out of his reflective space and back into the fading festivities of the ball, he did so with a renewed focus and determination. The night's experiences had equipped him with a deeper understanding of the nuances of success and the resilience required to pursue it. He was ready to face the challenges and embrace the opportunities that lay ahead in his journey.

As the Masked Ball drew to a close, Thabo stepped out into the cool Johannesburg night. The city lights twinkled like a constellation of dreams against the dark canvas of the sky, each light a story, a journey, a triumph. Standing there, Thabo felt a profound connection to the city and its myriad paths of success. The revelations of the evening resonated deeply within Thabo. The experience at the ball had been more than a mere social event; it had been a journey in itself, replete with lessons about the complexities of success. Thabo felt a renewed sense of purpose, his aspirations reinforced by the understanding that the path to success was lined with both accolades and challenges.

Rather than being deterred by the undercurrents of envy and rivalry he had witnessed, Thabo felt his resolve fortified. He recognized that achieving his goals would require resilience and a steadfast adherence to his values. The importance of integrity in his journey was clearer than ever. Thabo was determined to pursue his dreams while maintaining his ethical compass, regardless of the challenges he might face. As he walked away from the ball, Thabo's stride was confident, his mind alight with thoughts and plans.

The conversations and observations of the evening had given him a more nuanced perspective on success. He understood that his journey would not just be about technological innovations or professional achievements, but also about navigating the human elements that accompany success.

The night at the Masked Ball was a defining moment in Thabo's journey. It served as a bridge between his past and the future he was striving to create. As he looked at the sprawling city before him, he saw not just a landscape of buildings and lights, but a terrain of possibilities and opportunities. The chapter closes with Thabo taking a final look at the ballroom, now quiet and dimming, and then turning towards the city. With each step, he felt more connected to his journey, ready to face the intricacies of the path ahead. The lessons learned and the insights gained from the ball were now integral parts of him, guiding him as he stepped forward into the next chapter of his life.

PART 2: THE WEB OF DECEIT

SHADOWS IN CAPE TOWN"

As Thabo's journey progresses, his achievements and burgeoning reputation in the Johannesburg tech scene open the doors to a remarkable new opportunity. This chapter begins with Thabo stepping into a new phase of his career, one that promises to elevate his professional standing and challenge his abilities further. The chapter opens with Thabo receiving an invitation that would significantly alter the course of his career. A prestigious tech company in Cape Town, known for its innovative work in artificial intelligence, reaches out to him. They offer him the chance to collaborate on a ground-breaking project, one that is poised to make a significant impact in the tech industry.

The project, cantered around developing advanced AI solutions for environmental sustainability, is ambitious and aligns perfectly with Thabo's passion for using technology for social good. It represents not just a step forward in his career but also an opportunity to contribute to a cause he deeply cares about. Accepting this opportunity means a significant change for Thabo. He has to leave Johannesburg, his familiar professional network, and the comfort of his established routine. It's a decision that requires him to weigh his current success against the potential of even greater achievements and personal growth.

After much contemplation, Thabo decides to embrace this new challenge. He sees it as a chance to expand his horizons, to work with some of the brightest minds in the industry, and to be part of a project that could define the future of AI technology. The chapter continues with Thabo's arrival in Cape Town. The city, with its stunning landscapes and vibrant tech scene, is a blend of the familiar and the new. As he settles into this new environment, he feels a mix of excitement and anticipation for the work ahead.

Thabo's early days on the project are a whirlwind of learning and innovation. He is introduced to his team, a diverse group of talented individuals, each bringing unique skills and perspectives. The project's scope and potential excite Thabo, and he dives into his work with enthusiasm and dedication. As the chapter concludes, Thabo stands looking out over Cape Town's scenic coastline, reflecting on the journey that brought him here and the path that lies ahead. He feels a sense of accomplishment for how far he has come and a burgeoning curiosity for what this new chapter in Cape Town holds for him.

In "A New Opportunity in Cape Town," Thabo's journey takes a significant turn, introducing him to new challenges and opportunities that promise to shape his career and personal growth in profound ways. This chapter sets the stage for his continued evolution as a professional and as an individual in the ever-changing world of technology.

As Thabo stepped into the vibrant and multifaceted city of Cape Town, he found himself immersed in a world that was strikingly different from Johannesburg. This chapter explores Thabo's initial impressions of Cape Town, highlighting the city's unique blend of natural beauty and complex urban dynamics.

Thabo's first glimpse of Cape Town was one of awe-inspiring natural beauty. The city, nestled between the majestic Table Mountain and the vast expanse of the Atlantic Ocean, presented a picturesque panorama that was both serene and powerful. The sight of the mountain, with its peaks often draped in a 'tablecloth' of clouds, and the ocean, shimmering under the African sun, was a stark contrast to the urban landscape of Johannesburg.

As Thabo delved deeper into the city, he encountered the bustling energy of Cape Town's urban life. The city's tech hubs and business centres were alive with activity, pulsating with the energy of entrepreneurs, innovators, and professionals. The streets were a mix of modern architecture and historical buildings, each telling a story of the city's rich history and its rapid advancement into a cosmopolitan hub.

Cape Town's diverse cultural tapestry was another aspect that caught Thabo's attention. The city was a melting pot of cultures, each contributing to the rich fabric of society. From the colourful houses of Bo-Kaap to the lively markets of the city centre, each neighbourhood offered a different flavour of the city's diverse heritage.

However, as Thabo spent more time in the city, he began to discern the complex social dynamics beneath the surface. Cape Town, for all its beauty and progress, was also a city grappling with issues of inequality and historical divisions. The contrast between affluent neighbourhoods and underprivileged communities was more pronounced here, reflecting a city still navigating its past while looking toward the future.

Thabo realized that working in Cape Town would not just be a professional challenge but also a personal one. Adapting to the city's unique rhythm and understanding its social complexities would be essential to his success here. He was determined to immerse himself in the city, to learn from its people, and to contribute positively to its evolving story. As the chapter ends, Thabo stands on the shores of the city, looking out at the ocean, contemplating the confluence of beauty and complexity that is Cape Town. He is ready to embrace the city with all its contrasts, recognizing that it offers a new canvas for his aspirations and growth.

In "The Contrast of Cape Town," Thabo's arrival in the city marks the beginning of a new chapter in his life, one that promises to enrich him both professionally and personally. The chapter sets the scene for his upcoming experiences in a city that is as challenging as it is beautiful, offering a backdrop for his continued journey of growth and discovery.

Thabo's venture into the Cape Town tech scene introduces him to a new realm of professional dynamics, markedly different from his experiences in Johannesburg. This chapter delves into how Thabo adapts to and navigates these new settings, enhancing his understanding of the intricate world of business relationships and office politics.

Upon joining the Cape Town project, Thabo is introduced to a network of professionals who are well-versed in the tech industry's nuances. He notices that the interactions here are more refined and calculated. Conversations are laced with subtlety, and professional moves are made with careful consideration, revealing a more sophisticated approach to business dealings.

Thabo observes that the business culture in Cape Town is characterized by a polished exterior. Meetings are conducted with a degree of formality, and presentations are meticulously prepared. The professionals he meets are adept at presenting their ideas and themselves, showcasing a blend of style and substance.

As Thabo becomes more involved in the project, he begins to see the strategic nature of professional alliances. Partnerships and collaborations are carefully chosen for mutual benefit, and networking events are opportunities to forge potentially advantageous connections.

Thabo learns to approach these alliances with a blend of openness and caution, aware of their potential impact on his work and career. One of the more challenging aspects Thabo faces is understanding the underlying rivalries.

Unlike the more overt competition he was used to in Johannesburg, the rivalries in Cape Town are subtle and often hidden behind a veneer of professionalism. He learns to read between the lines in meetings and discussions, picking up on the subtle cues that indicate competitive undercurrents.

Thabo quickly realizes that to succeed in this new environment, he must adapt his approach. He hopes his communication skills to be more diplomatic and learns to navigate the intricate web of relationships with tact and discernment. He also becomes more mindful of his actions and decisions, understanding their potential ripple effects in the interconnected professional network. Throughout this experience, Thabo remains committed to maintaining his integrity. He resolves to navigate the office politics without compromising his values, believing that honest work and ethical conduct will stand him in good stead.

The chapter concludes with Thabo reflecting on the complexities of the new professional dynamics he's encountered. He recognizes that navigating these waters is a delicate balancing act – one that requires a blend of astuteness, integrity, and adaptability. Armed with these insights, Thabo is ready to face the challenges and opportunities that this new environment presents. In "Navigating New Professional Dynamics," Thabo encounters and learns to manage the sophisticated and strategic nature of professional relationships in Cape Town. This chapter portrays his growth as he adapts to these new dynamics, becoming more adept at understanding and navigating the complex web of professional interactions.

Thabo's deeper involvement in the Cape Town project brings him face-to-face with the more insidious aspects of professional life. This chapter explores his encounters with deceit and betrayal, skilfully masked by the polished veneer of professional interactions. Thabo, with his earnest approach and genuine enthusiasm for the project, initially sees his new colleagues as allies.

However, as he delves deeper, he begins to notice discrepancies between their words and actions. Colleagues who appeared friendly and helpful at first start to show a different side. Their charm and affability, he realizes, are sometimes tools to mask true intentions.

In team meetings and collaborations, Thabo encounters situations where the interests of others are not as transparent as they seem. He learns that behind the collaborative facade, some are manoeuvring for their gain, using the project as a stepping stone for personal ambitions. This revelation is a stark contrast to Thabo's straightforward approach to teamwork and shared success.

As these experiences accumulate, Thabo becomes more adept at reading subtle cues and understanding the undercurrents of office politics. He starts to discern which colleagues are genuinely supportive and which ones are motivated by self-interest. This newfound discernment is a crucial skill in navigating the complex terrain of the project.

The turning point comes when Thabo uncovers a plot by a colleague to take credit for his work. This act of betrayal, executed with a careful strategy to avoid suspicion, is a jarring experience for Thabo. It forces him to confront the reality that the professional world can be rife with deceit, especially when high stakes are involved. Armed with these hard-earned insights, Thabo adopts a more cautious approach in his professional dealings.

He learns to protect his work, communicate strategically, and build alliances with those he trusts. This careful navigation, however, does not dampen his commitment to the project or his passion for technology.

As the chapter closes, Thabo reflects on the lessons learned from encountering subtle deceit. These experiences, though challenging, have honed his ability to navigate complex professional landscapes. He emerges from these encounters more vigilant and astute, yet undeterred in his pursuit of innovation and success. "Encountering Subtle Deceit" presents a significant phase in Thabo's journey, where he learns the intricate and sometimes dark aspects of professional relationships. This chapter highlights his growth in discernment and strategic thinking, essential skills for his continued success in the competitive world of technology.

Thabo's journey, he faces a stark betrayal that serves as a profound lesson in the realities of corporate deception and tests the very foundations of his trust and resilience. The revelation comes unexpectedly. Thabo, while reviewing project documents, stumbles upon discrepancies that lead him to a troubling discovery. A colleague, whom he had considered a mentor and ally, had been subtly manipulating his work. This colleague, skilled in the art of corporate politics, had been passing Thabo's ideas as their own and slowly steering the project in a direction that undermined Thabo's contributions.

Thabo's initial reaction is one of disbelief. The colleague had always been supportive, offering guidance and encouragement. The realization that this support was a facade for deceit is a jarring experience. Thabo confronts the colleague, seeking explanations. The confrontation, however, is met with denial and evasion, adding to Thabo's disillusionment.

As Thabo reflects on the events leading up to the discovery, he begins to piece together the motives behind the betrayal. He realizes that the colleague's actions were driven by a desire to control the project's direction and gain recognition at the expense of others. This insight into the darker side of professional ambition is a sobering moment for Thabo.

This betrayal tests Thabo's resilience like never before. He grapples with feelings of anger, disappointment, and a sense of betrayal. However, Thabo refuses to let this experience embitter him. Instead, he channels his emotions into a renewed focus on his work, determined not to let the deceit of one individual derail his goals. Thabo emerges from this experience more cautious and aware of the complexities of workplace relationships. He learns to safeguard his work and ideas and to build a network of trust based on proven actions rather than words. This incident, though painful, becomes a valuable lesson in vigilance and discernment.

Thabo reflects on the ordeal with a sense of sober maturity. The betrayal, while a harsh lesson, has not diminished his passion or commitment. Instead, it has equipped him with a more realistic understanding of the corporate world. Thabo moves forward with a strengthened resolve, more resilient and prepared for the challenges that lie ahead. "A Betrayal Unveiled" is a turning point in Thabo's narrative, marking a shift in his understanding of corporate dynamics and trust. It portrays his ability to withstand and learn from difficult experiences, shaping him into a more astute and resilient professional.

In the aftermath of the betrayal, Thabo finds himself in a period of introspection and growth. This chapter captures his journey of learning from the shadows of deceit, as he develops a deeper understanding of the complexities of professional interactions and the importance of vigilance. The betrayal serves as a catalyst for Thabo to hone his ability to discern true intentions. He becomes more observant of people's behaviours and communication styles, learning to pick up on subtle cues that may indicate underlying motives. Thabo understands that in the corporate world, not all intentions are transparent, and being able to discern these nuances is crucial.

Thabo starts to approach meetings and discussions with a new perspective. He learns to read between the lines, understanding that what is unsaid can often be as important as what is spoken. This skill helps him navigate conversations more effectively, ensuring he is not misled or blindsided by hidden agendas.

Realizing the importance of protecting his work and ideas, Thabo adopts a more guarded professional persona. While he remains collaborative and open to genuine teamwork, he becomes more strategic about sharing information and more selective in forming professional alliances.

One of Thabo's significant learnings is finding the balance between trust and caution. He understands that while it's essential to build relationships based on trust, it's equally important to maintain a level of caution, especially in new or untested professional relationships. Thabo reflects on how this experience, although difficult, has been instrumental in his professional growth. He recognizes that such challenges are part of the journey and embracing the lessons they bring is essential for personal and career development.

As the chapter concludes, Thabo emerges as a more astute and cautious professional. He has learned to navigate the shadows of the corporate world with a new level of awareness and sophistication. This experience, while a shadow in his career, has illuminated essential truths about the professional world and fortified his resolve to succeed with integrity and foresight. "Learning from the Shadows" explores Thabo's growth in the wake of professional betrayal, highlighting his development into a more discerning and strategic professional. This chapter underscores the importance of learning from adversity, a theme that resonates with Thabo's overall journey of growth and success.

Thabo's challenging experiences in Cape Town have not only tested but also fortified his professional resolve. The betrayals and deceptions Thabo faced in Cape Town, while initially disheartening, ultimately serve as a crucible for his growth. He emerges from these experiences with a heightened sense of astuteness and a more nuanced understanding of the professional landscape. These trials have sharpened his ability to discern true intentions and navigate complex relationships.

Thabo's journey in Cape Town teaches him the delicate balance between idealism and realism in the professional world. He retains his core values and aspirations but now approaches his career with a more pragmatic outlook. This balance ensures that he remains true to his vision while being aware of the realities of the corporate environment. The chapter highlights Thabo's strengthened emotional resilience. The setbacks he encounters do not diminish his passion or drive; instead, they reinforce his determination to succeed. This resilience is a testament to Thabo's character and his commitment to his goals.

Equipped with new insights and skills, Thabo is more prepared than ever to face future challenges. He understands that the road to success is fraught with obstacles, but he is now better equipped to overcome them. His experiences in Cape Town have provided him with valuable tools that will aid him in future endeavours.

As Thabo prepares to move forward, he does so with a renewed determination to succeed. He is no longer the naïve professional who first arrived in Cape Town; he is a more seasoned and strategic thinker, ready to take on the complexities of the tech industry.

The chapter ends with Thabo gazing out over Cape Town's skyline, reflecting on his journey. He feels a sense of accomplishment for the growth he has achieved and a sense of anticipation for what lies ahead. With a strengthened resolve and a deepened understanding of the professional world, Thabo is ready to continue his journey, embracing whatever challenges and opportunities the future holds.

The conclusion of this chapter marks a pivotal point in Thabo's professional journey, underscoring his evolution into a more seasoned, resilient, and strategic professional. His experiences in Cape Town, though fraught with challenges, pave the way for his continued success and growth in the tech industry.

In a modern boardroom in Cape Town, overlooking the bustling city. The atmosphere is charged with anticipation as Thabo and his team members gather for a crucial meeting to review the progress of their high-profile tech project. Thabo, armed with months of hard work and ground-breaking findings, is prepared to showcase his contributions to the project. His presentation, meticulously crafted, is set to highlight the innovative solutions he developed, solutions that could significantly advance the project's objectives.

The room is filled with key stakeholders and senior members of the tech company, all eager to assess the project's progress. The air is thick with expectation as the meeting commences. Thabo patiently waits for his turn to present, confident in the value of his work and its impact on the project. As the meeting progresses, a senior colleague, someone Thabo had viewed as a mentor and ally, takes the floor. To Thabo's utter disbelief, this colleague begins to present Thabo's findings as their own. They articulate the strategies and solutions Thabo had developed, leaving no room for doubt that they are claiming full ownership of his work.

Thabo is blindsided by this betrayal. He feels a mix of shock, anger, and disbelief. The trust and respect he had for this colleague shatter in an instant. He grapples with the realization that his work, the product of countless hours of dedication, is being usurped right in front of him. In this moment of betrayal, Thabo faces a dilemma. Does he confront the situation head-on in the meeting, risking a professional scene, or does he seek a more strategic approach to address this injustice? The decision is complex, weighed down by the potential implications of each course of action.

As the colleague concludes their presentation to applause and accolades, Thabo sits in quiet turmoil. The meeting moves on, but Thabo's mind is racing, formulating a response to this unexpected turn of events.

The opening of "Betrayal in the Boardroom" sets a dramatic tone for the chapter, depicting a critical moment in Thabo's career where he faces a profound professional betrayal. This moment serves as a catalyst for the unfolding events of the chapter, challenging Thabo's resilience and integrity in the face of deception.

Thabo is engulfed in a tumult of emotions, grappling with the stark reality of the betrayal he has just experienced. The revelation hits Thabo like a physical blow. He sits in stunned silence, trying to process what he has just witnessed. The colleague he had admired and trusted, who had been a guiding figure in his professional journey, had just blatantly presented his ideas and hard work as their own. The sense of shock is overwhelming, leaving Thabo momentarily paralyzed.

As the shock begins to subside, disbelief takes its place. Thabo finds himself questioning the reality of the situation. He replays the moments of the presentation in his mind, hoping to find an explanation or a misunderstanding, but the truth remains unchanged. The betrayal is clear and undeniable. The feeling of betrayal sinks in deeply. Thabo reflects on the countless hours he spent confiding in and seeking advice from this colleague, now realizing that his trust was misplaced. The mentor figure he had looked up to had exploited his trust for personal gain, leaving Thabo feeling deceived and used.

Despite the turmoil raging within him, Thabo knows he must maintain his composure in the professional setting of the boardroom. He struggles to keep his emotions in check, maintaining a calm exterior while his mind races with thoughts of injustice and frustration. As the meeting adjourns and colleagues begin to leave the room, Thabo remains seated, trying to gather his thoughts. The reality of what has transpired is hard to accept, and he feels a profound sense of isolation amidst the people who were once his team.

The chapter concludes with Thabo seeking a moment of solitude to reflect on the events. He steps away from the boardroom, finding a quiet spot where he can be alone with his thoughts. The initial shock and disbelief gradually give way to a determination to address the situation. Thabo realizes that he must find a way to reclaim his work and confront the betrayal, but the path forward is fraught with uncertainty. "Shock and Disbelief" captures the intense emotional impact of the betrayal Thabo experiences in the boardroom. This section of the chapter sets the stage for his response to this profound professional and personal challenge, highlighting his inner strength and the beginning of his resolve to seek justice and uphold his integrity.

In the wake of the shocking revelation in the boardroom, Thabo finds himself navigating a storm of emotions and decisions, trying to find the best way forward in the aftermath of the betrayal. As Thabo steps out of the boardroom, he is engulfed in a maelstrom of feelings.

Anger at the betrayal, a deep sense of injustice, and a feeling of helplessness swirl within him. He had poured his heart and intellect into the project, only to have his work claimed by someone he trusted. Thabo's initial instinct is to confront the situation head-on, to call out the betrayal in front of his colleagues and demand justice. The urge to react impulsively, to give voice to his anger and sense of injustice, is strong. He yearns for immediate vindication.

However, as he takes a moment to breathe and reflect, Thabo realizes the potential consequences of a hasty reaction. He understands that handling the situation impulsively could harm his professional reputation and possibly jeopardize his position in the project and the company. The stakes are high, and every action he takes needs to be calculated and deliberate.

Drawing upon a reservoir of inner strength, Thabo decides to maintain his composure. Despite the turmoil raging inside him, he presents a calm exterior. He greets his colleagues with a nod as he leaves the boardroom, masking the turmoil within. This display of self-control, though difficult, is a testament to Thabo's professionalism and maturity.

Thabo seeks solace in the quiet of his office. There, he allows himself to process the emotions fully, to confront the anger and betrayal in a space where he can think clearly. It's in this solitude that Thabo begins to formulate a plan. He starts to consider his options, to strategize on how best to address the betrayal and reclaim his work. Thabo emerges from his reflection with a clearer mind. He recognizes that the path ahead will be challenging but is determined to navigate it with dignity and strategy. The immediate fallout of the betrayal has been a test of his character, one that he has met with composure and a resolve to seek justice in a measured, thoughtful manner.

"Navigating the Immediate Fallout" portrays Thabo's immediate emotional response to the betrayal and his decision to handle the situation with composure and strategic thinking. This part of the chapter sets the stage for the actions he will take to address the injustice and reclaim his rightful place in the project. Thabo embarks on a quest for resolution, armed with evidence and a determination to reclaim his work. This section of the chapter explores his strategic approach to addressing the injustice he has faced.

Thabo's first step is to meticulously gather evidence of his contributions to the project. He compiles emails, documents, and presentations that clearly demonstrate his work and ideas. This process is painstaking but necessary, as Thabo knows that he needs solid proof to support his claims. Thabo spends time analysing the situation, understanding the dynamics at play. He reflects on the motivations behind the betrayal and considers the best approach to address it. This analysis helps him in strategizing his next steps, ensuring that his actions are calculated and effective.

Knowing that the company's hierarchy and internal politics could influence the outcome, Thabo carefully plans his approach. He decides to first seek a private meeting with the colleague who betrayed him, hoping for a resolution that doesn't escalate the situation. However, he also prepares for the possibility of taking the matter to higher management. Thabo arranges a meeting with the colleague, presenting his evidence and expressing his feelings of betrayal. The conversation is tense, with the colleague initially defensive. Thabo remains firm yet professional, making it clear that he expects recognition for his work and an appropriate resolution.

When it becomes apparent that the colleague is not willing to rectify the situation, Thabo takes the bold step of escalating the matter to higher management. He presents his case calmly and objectively, supported by the evidence he has collected. This step is fraught with risk, but Thabo feels it's necessary to stand up for his work and integrity. After presenting his case, Thabo finds himself in a period of waiting. The decision is now in the hands of the company's higher management. This waiting period is challenging, filled with uncertainty and anxiety, but Thabo remains hopeful that justice will prevail.

Thabo reflects on the steps he has taken. He recognizes that seeking resolution has been a test of his patience, courage, and professionalism. Regardless of the outcome, he takes solace in the fact that he has stood up for himself and acted with integrity in the face of adversity. "Seeking Resolution" highlights Thabo's proactive and strategic approach to addressing a significant professional betrayal. This part of the chapter underscores his resilience and commitment to justice, setting the stage for the resolution of this critical conflict in his career.

As Thabo navigates the difficult aftermath of the betrayal, his resilience becomes a central theme. This section of the chapter delves into how he copes with and overcomes the adversity he faces. Confronted with one of the most challenging situations of his career, Thabo taps into a deep well of inner strength. He reminds himself of the obstacles he has overcome in the past and the personal growth he has achieved. This introspection provides him with the fortitude to face the current challenge head-on.

Thabo reflects on the lessons learned from his previous encounters with deceit and betrayal. These experiences, though painful, have equipped him with a better understanding of the corporate world's complexities. He uses these insights to navigate the current situation with a more strategic and level-headed approach. Despite the turmoil, Thabo remains steadfastly committed to his work. He continues to contribute to the project with the same dedication and passion as before, refusing to let the actions of others diminish his professionalism or work quality.

Thabo experiences a range of emotions, from anger and frustration to disappointment. However, he consciously chooses not to let these emotions overpower him. He finds healthy outlets for his feelings, such as talking to trusted friends or engaging in physical activities, which help him maintain emotional balance. Recognizing the value of support, Thabo reaches out to mentors and colleagues for guidance. Their advice and empathy provide him with additional perspectives and strategies to handle the situation, reinforcing his resolve.

Throughout this ordeal, Thabo holds firmly to his integrity and values. He refuses to retaliate with underhanded tactics, believing that upholding his principles is more important than a short-term victory. As the section concludes, Thabo stands as a testament to resilience in the face of adversity. He has not only managed to navigate the immediate fallout of the betrayal but has also grown stronger and more resilient. This experience, though difficult, has honed his ability to withstand professional challenges and emerge with his integrity intact. "Resilience in the Face of Adversity" portrays Thabo's ability to withstand and learn from a significant professional setback. This part of the chapter highlights his emotional and professional strength, setting a powerful example of resilience in the face of challenging circumstances.

As Thabo navigates the difficult aftermath of the betrayal, his resilience becomes a central theme. This section of the chapter delves into how he copes with and overcomes the adversity he faces. Confronted with one of the most challenging situations of his career, Thabo taps into a deep well of inner strength. He reminds himself of the obstacles he has overcome in the past and the personal growth he has achieved. This introspection provides him with the fortitude to face the current challenge head-on.

Thabo reflects on the lessons learned from his previous encounters with deceit and betrayal. These experiences, though painful, have equipped him with a better understanding of the corporate world's complexities. He uses these insights to navigate the current situation with a more strategic and level-headed approach. Despite the turmoil, Thabo remains steadfastly committed to his work. He continues to contribute to the project with the same dedication and passion as before, refusing to let the actions of others diminish his professionalism or work quality.

Thabo experiences a range of emotions, from anger and frustration to disappointment. However, he consciously chooses not to let these emotions overpower him. He finds healthy outlets for his feelings, such as talking to trusted friends or engaging in physical activities, which help him maintain emotional balance.

Recognizing the value of support, Thabo reaches out to mentors and colleagues for guidance. Their advice and empathy provide him with additional perspectives and strategies to handle the situation, reinforcing his resolve.

Throughout this ordeal, Thabo holds firmly to his integrity and values. He refuses to retaliate with underhanded tactics, believing that upholding his principles is more important than a short-term victory. As the section concludes, Thabo stands as a testament to resilience in the face of adversity. He has not only managed to navigate the immediate fallout of the betrayal but has also grown stronger and more resilient. This experience, though difficult, has honed his ability to withstand professional challenges and emerge with his integrity intact.

"Resilience in the Face of Adversity" portrays Thabo's ability to withstand and learn from a significant professional setback. This part of the chapter highlights his emotional and professional strength, setting a powerful example of resilience in the face of challenging circumstances.

In the face of the profound betrayal in the boardroom, Thabo confronts a crucial test of his character and integrity. This section of the chapter explores how he navigates this moral dilemma, upholding his principles while addressing the injustice.

Faced with a situation that could easily provoke a less measured response, Thabo chooses to handle the matter with utmost professionalism. He realizes that any impulsive or emotionally charged reaction could compromise his standing and principles. This decision to remain composed and rational, even in the heat of the moment, speaks volumes about his character.

The betrayal naturally evokes feelings of anger and a desire for retribution. Thabo grapples with these emotions, recognizing the ease with which he could retaliate or expose the betrayer in a public setting. However, he understands that such actions would only perpetuate a cycle of unethical behaviour and ultimately harm his integrity. Throughout the ordeal, Thabo displays grace under pressure. He manages to articulate his concerns and present his evidence without resorting to personal attacks or unprofessional conduct. This approach not only strengthens his case but also earns him respect from his peers and superiors.

Thabo's response to the betrayal reinforces his commitment to ethical standards in the workplace. He stands by his belief that success should not be achieved at the cost of one's values. This commitment to integrity, even when it might be easier to abandon it, is a defining aspect of his character.

In his pursuit of resolution, Thabo focuses on seeking justice rather than revenge. He aims to rectify the situation and restore his rightful recognition, but not at the expense of his moral compass. This distinction is crucial in maintaining his self-respect and professional dignity.

As the section concludes, Thabo emerges not only as a victim of betrayal but more importantly, as a figure of strength and integrity. His response to the betrayal highlights his moral fortitude, proving that one's character is not defined by the challenges they face, but by how they choose to respond to them. "A Test of Character and Integrity" emphasizes Thabo's ethical response to a challenging professional situation, underscoring the strength of his character and his commitment to maintaining high standards of professionalism and integrity. This part of the chapter sets a powerful example of ethical conduct in the face of adversity.

This concludes with a resolution that marks a significant turning point in Thabo's professional journey. The trials he has faced and overcome in this chapter have not only tested his resilience but have also contributed to his growth as a professional. Thabo's steadfast efforts to seek justice and reclaim his work pay off. The evidence he presents and the case he makes to the higher management lead to a recognition of his true contributions to the project.

The truth about the betrayal is acknowledged, and Thabo's work is rightfully attributed to him, restoring his professional standing and reputation.

This experience, though fraught with challenges, has been a profound learning opportunity for Thabo. He gains a deeper understanding of corporate ethics and the importance of navigating professional relationships with caution and discernment. These lessons are invaluable and will guide him in his future endeavours. Emerging from this ordeal, Thabo feels a renewed sense of purpose and clarity about his career path. The adversity has reinforced his belief in the value of integrity and ethical conduct in the workplace. He is more committed than ever to pursue his professional goals with honesty and transparency.

The chapter highlights Thabo's strengthened resilience. The manner in which he handles the betrayal - with grace, professionalism, and integrity - demonstrates his ability to withstand and overcome professional challenges. This resilience is a testament to his character and will be a key asset in his future career.

As Thabo prepares to continue his journey, he does so with a heightened awareness of the complexities of the corporate world and a stronger resolve to navigate these challenges. He looks towards the future with confidence, ready to embrace new opportunities and face any obstacles with the same determination and integrity that have brought him this far.

The chapter closes with Thabo reflecting on his journey, acknowledging the growth he has experienced through this challenging episode. He stands ready to embark on the next phase of his career, equipped with new insights, a stronger sense of self, and an unwavering commitment to his principles.

The conclusion of "Betrayal in the Boardroom" sees Thabo emerging stronger and more resilient, having navigated a significant professional challenge. This resolution sets the stage for the next chapter of his career, highlighting his growth and readiness to face future challenges with a renewed sense of purpose and integrity.

PART 3: THE BATTLE WITHIN

REFLECTIONS IN THE STORM

After the tumultuous events in Cape Town, Thabo seeks a respite for introspection and healing. He chooses to retreat to one of South Africa's serene locales – the majestic Drakensberg Mountains – a setting that provides the perfect backdrop for contemplation and self-discovery. Thabo's journey to the Drakensberg Mountains symbolizes his transition from the tumultuous corporate world to a realm of peace and natural beauty, offering him a much-needed respite and space for reflection.

Thabo leaving the bustling streets of Cape Town. As he drives away from the city, he feels a sense of relief, the weight of the boardroom betrayal beginning to lift. The urban landscapes, with their skyscrapers and constant movement, gradually fade in his rear-view mirror, signalling the end of one chapter and the beginning of another. As Thabo approaches the Drakensberg region, he is greeted by the awe-inspiring sight of the mountains. The Drakensberg range, known for its majestic beauty, stands tall and imposing, a testament to the enduring power of nature. The rugged peaks and expansive valleys, draped in hues of green and brown, present a stark contrast to the concrete and glass of the city.

Thabo finds himself enveloped in the tranquillity of the Drakensberg. The air is fresher, the sounds of nature more pronounced, and the pace of life noticeably slower. He takes deep breaths, allowing the clean mountain air to fill his lungs, feeling the stress and tension of recent events ebb away. As he hikes through the mountain trails, Thabo is captivated by the grandeur of the Drakensberg. The towering cliffs, cascading waterfalls, and verdant forests are a balm to his troubled mind. The vastness of the landscape puts his problems into perspective, reminding him of the wider world beyond the confines of office walls. Thabo spends a night camping under the star-filled sky, the silence of the mountains around him. As he gazes up at the twinkling stars, he feels a sense of connection to the universe, a feeling that his struggles, while significant, are part of a larger tapestry of life.

The chapter section concludes with Thabo waking up to a stunning sunrise over the mountains. The beauty and peace of the Drakensberg have begun their healing work on him. He feels a renewed sense of hope and strength, ready to delve into introspection and re-evaluate his life's priorities away from the pressures of the corporate world. "The Journey to Drakensberg" in "Reflections in the Storm" serves as a metaphorical passage for Thabo, leading him from a world of turmoil to one of peace and natural splendour. This journey sets the stage for a period of introspection and personal growth amid the beauty and serenity of the Drakensberg Mountains.

Thabo's time in the Drakensberg Mountains becomes a journey of self-discovery, as he immerses himself in the solitude and raw beauty of the landscape. This section of the chapter explores how nature becomes a catalyst for Thabo's introspection and healing. The serene environment of the Drakensberg offers Thabo a much-needed escape from the complexities of his professional life. Surrounded by the majestic beauty of the mountains, he finds a sense of peace and solace that had eluded him in the city. The solitude allows him to disconnect from the outside world and turn his focus inward.

As Thabo hikes through the rugged terrain, with its vast open spaces and towering peaks, he gains a new perspective on his life's troubles. The immensity of the landscape reminds him of the vastness of the world and the relative smallness of individual concerns. This realization brings a sense of humility and clarity, helping him to see his recent experiences in a broader context.

The solitude of the Drakensberg becomes a backdrop for deep reflection. Thabo contemplates his journey so far – the successes, the setbacks, and the lessons learned. He thinks about his values, his aspirations, and what truly matters to him. This time of reflection is introspective and transformative, allowing Thabo to reconnect with his core beliefs and aspirations. The natural beauty of the Drakensberg not only offers visual splendour but also aids in Thabo's emotional healing. The act of hiking, the rhythm of his steps, and the tranquillity of the surroundings work together to soothe his mind. He finds that each day in the mountains brings a gradual release of the tensions and disappointments that had built up.

In the heart of nature, Thabo begins to rediscover parts of himself that had been overshadowed by his professional endeavours. He rediscovers his love for nature, the joy of solitude, and the importance of balancing life's various aspects. This rediscovery is empowering, giving him a renewed sense of self and purpose. As this section of the chapter closes, Thabo stands atop a high peak, looking out over the sprawling landscape of the Drakensberg. He feels a deep connection to the natural world and a renewed appreciation for life's journey, with all its twists and turns. The solitude and beauty of nature have provided him with the space to heal and grow, readying him to return to his professional life with a refreshed spirit and a clearer mind.

"Embracing Solitude and Nature" in "Reflections in the Storm" highlights Thabo's journey of self-healing and introspection amidst the stunning backdrop of the Drakensberg Mountains. This experience becomes a turning point in his life, allowing him to find peace and gain a renewed perspective on his personal and professional paths. In the serene embrace of the Drakensberg, Thabo finds the clarity and space to engage in a profound exploration of his personal values, a journey that reshapes his understanding of success and fulfilment.

Amidst the quietude of nature, Thabo begins to question the conventional definitions of success that are often tied to career advancements, accolades, and material gain. He reflects on his own aspirations and the driving forces behind them, pondering whether his pursuit of success has been aligned with his true self. Thabo delves deep into understanding his core values. He realizes that while professional success is important, it is not the sole marker of a fulfilling life. He acknowledges the value of relationships, personal growth, and making a positive impact on others and the world around him.

The recent betrayal and its aftermath have made Thabo acutely aware of the importance of integrity and ethics in both personal and professional spheres. He reaffirms his commitment to uphold these values, recognizing that true success is not just about what is achieved, but also how it is achieved. Thabo contemplates the balance between his professional ambitions and personal life. He acknowledges that his focus on career goals had sometimes come at the expense of other aspects of his life. This introspection leads him to resolve to seek a more harmonious balance, ensuring that his work enriches rather than detracts from his overall life experience.

Through his reflections, Thabo arrives at a more personal and holistic definition of success. For him, success encompasses not only achieving professional goals but also living authentically, nurturing relationships, and contributing positively to society. He realizes that success is a personal journey, unique to each individual.

As the section concludes, Thabo emerges from his introspective journey with a renewed outlook on life and success. He feels more aligned with his true self, equipped with a clearer vision of how he wants to shape his future. The tranquillity of the Drakensberg has provided him with a valuable opportunity to realign his life's path with his deepest values and aspirations.

In the peaceful backdrop of the Drakensberg Mountains, Thabo embarks on a journey to redefine the meaning of success, an introspection that challenges his previous perceptions and priorities. Amid the quietude of the mountains, Thabo reflects on his earlier career-centric view of success. He realizes that while professional achievements are fulfilling, they represent just one aspect of a successful life. He starts to question if his relentless pursuit of career goals has overshadowed other important elements of personal fulfilment.

Thabo expands his understanding of success beyond the confines of professional achievements. He contemplates the significance of personal growth, emotional well-being, and the richness of relationships. The realization dawns on him that true success is multi-dimensional, involving not just what he accomplishes but also who he becomes in the process. In the solitude of nature, Thabo appreciates the value of relationships and community.

He reflects on how meaningful connections with family, friends, and the community contribute to a sense of success and fulfilment. He recognizes the importance of nurturing these relationships as part of a well-rounded and successful life.

Thabo also considers the impact of his work on society. He ponders whether success entails contributing positively to the world and leaving a meaningful legacy. This reflection leads him to consider aligning his professional endeavours with causes that benefit society and the environment. Thabo comes to understand that success is a personal concept, unique to each individual. He realizes that defining success on his own terms is crucial and that it should align with his values, passions, and purpose. This understanding frees him from societal pressures and expectations, allowing him to chart his own path.

As this section of the chapter concludes, Thabo gazes out over the vast expanse of the Drakensberg, feeling a sense of clarity and peace. He has come to a new understanding of success, one that encompasses professional achievements as well as personal growth, relationships, and social contribution. With this holistic view of success, Thabo is ready to approach his life and career with a renewed sense of purpose and fulfilment. "Understanding the Meaning of Success" in "Reflections in the Storm" captures Thabo's evolving perspective on success. This introspective journey in the serenity of the Drakensberg leads him to a more holistic and personal definition of success, one that resonates with his values and aspirations.

Amidst the majestic tranquillity of the Drakensberg, Thabo embarks on a journey of self-reconnection, rediscovering aspects of himself that had been overshadowed by his professional pursuits. In the solitude of the mountains, Thabo finds the space to step away from his professional identity. Away from the demands and the constant striving for success, he begins to see himself not just as a professional but as a whole person with varied interests and passions.

Thabo rediscovers hobbies and interests that he had neglected in the pursuit of his career. He finds joy in activities like photography, capturing the breath-taking landscapes of the Drakensberg, and journaling, where he pens his thoughts and reflections. These activities, once a vital part of his life, rekindle a sense of creativity and happiness that had been dimmed by his professional obligations.

The natural beauty of the Drakensberg plays a significant role in Thabo's rediscovery of his inner self. He finds peace in the simple pleasures of nature – the serene sunrises, the quiet of the night sky, and the melodies of the wilderness. This connection with nature brings a sense of harmony and balance to his life.

Thabo takes this time to reflect on his personal values and what they mean to him. He contemplates the qualities he wants to embody, such as kindness, empathy, and authenticity. This reflection helps him align his actions with these values, ensuring that his life path is true to who he is at his core. This retreat also highlights the importance of self-care for Thabo. He realizes that taking care of his mental and emotional well-being is crucial for a fulfilling life. This understanding prompts him to commit to making self-care a regular part of his routine.

As Thabo prepares to leave the Drakensberg, he does so with a renewed sense of self. He has reconnected with parts of himself that he had lost in the whirlwind of his career. This reconnection has not only rejuvenated him but also given him a clearer understanding of what he seeks in life, both professionally and personally. "Reconnecting with Inner Self" in "Reflections in the Storm" is a pivotal section that highlights Thabo's journey of self-reconnection and rediscovery. This period of solitude and reflection enables him to realign with his passions, interests, and values, contributing to a more balanced and fulfilling life.

The concluding section of "Reflections in the Storm" captures Thabo's transformation following his introspective journey in the Drakensberg. He emerges with a newfound clarity and determination that reshapes his approach to both his professional and personal life.

Thabo's time in the Drakensberg allows him to redefine his concept of success. He now views success not just in terms of professional achievements but as a more holistic measure that includes personal fulfilment, ethical integrity, and contributing positively to society. This broader perspective of success will guide his future endeavours.

With his newfound clarity, Thabo is ready to re-engage with the corporate world, but with a different mindset. He is determined to pursue projects and roles that not only advance his career but also align with his personal values and the greater good. This approach ensures that his work is not only rewarding in a professional sense but also meaningful on a personal level. Thabo's experience in the Drakensberg reinforces his commitment to living according to his values. He resolves to maintain his integrity, uphold his ethical standards, and nurture the relationships that enrich his life. This commitment is a guiding light in his decision-making process, both at work and in his personal life.

Thabo returns with a renewed commitment to balancing his professional ambitions with his personal well-being. He understands the importance of self-care, leisure, and spending time with loved ones, recognizing that a fulfilling life is about balance. The challenges and betrayals Thabo faced have equipped him with resilience and a more strategic approach to handling workplace dynamics. He is prepared to face future challenges with a calm and measured response, drawing on the lessons and strength he gained from his time in the Drakensberg.

As Thabo leaves the serenity of the Drakensberg and heads back to the hustle of the city, he feels ready for the new beginnings that await him. He steps into the next chapter of his life with a clear vision, renewed energy, and a resolve to live and work in a way that is true to himself. The conclusion marks a significant turning point in Thabo's narrative, showcasing his growth and readiness to embrace his professional and personal life with a new perspective. His experiences in the Drakensberg serve as a foundation for a more mindful and value-driven approach to his future path.

RETURN TO JOHANNESBURG: A CHANGED PERSPECTIVE

After his transformative experience in the Drakensberg, Thabo returns to Johannesburg with a renewed sense of self and purpose. This chapter explores how his new insights and resolve reshape his approach to his professional life and relationships in the bustling city. Thabo's journey back to Johannesburg signifies a return to his professional life, but with a new outlook shaped by his time of introspection in the Drakensberg.

As Thabo drives through the streets of Johannesburg, the cityscape that once felt overwhelmingly fast-paced and demanding now presents itself differently. The skyscrapers, bustling traffic, and vibrant urban life, though unchanged physically, evoke new feelings and thoughts in him. He sees the city not just as a place of professional challenges but as a landscape filled with opportunities for growth and contribution.

Pausing at a traffic light, Thabo takes a moment to reflect on his journey. He recalls the serenity of the Drakensberg and the clarity it brought him. This moment of stillness amidst the city's hustle allows him to reconcile his past experiences with his present state, acknowledging the growth he has undergone.

Thabo feels a sense of anticipation as he considers the possibilities that lie ahead. He is eager to apply the insights and resolutions he gained during his retreat to his professional endeavours. This anticipation is tempered with a sense of calm, a stark contrast to the anxiety he once felt in the face of uncertainty.

As he navigates the streets, Thabo embraces Johannesburg's complexity with a new perspective. He recognizes the city's dynamic energy as a driving force that can inspire innovation and resilience. The challenges that once seemed daunting are now viewed as stepping stones for personal and professional development.

For Thabo, Johannesburg becomes a canvas for applying his newfound perspectives. He sees opportunities to integrate his personal values into his professional life, to foster meaningful relationships, and to contribute positively to the city's tech community. As this section concludes, Thabo arrives at his destination, feeling a renewed connection with Johannesburg. The city, once a symbol of relentless ambition, now represents a balanced approach to life and career. Thabo steps out of his car, ready to engage with his familiar surroundings with a refreshed mindset and a clear vision for the future.

"Back to the Urban Landscape" in "Return to Johannesburg: A Changed Perspective" highlights Thabo's re-entry into his professional environment with a renewed sense of purpose and understanding.

His contemplative journey back to the city sets the tone for how he plans to navigate his career and personal life with his newly gained insights. Thabo's return to Johannesburg marks the beginning of a new chapter in his professional life, characterized by a deliberate and values-driven approach to his career.

With a newfound understanding of success, Thabo re-evaluates his professional goals. He now prioritizes projects not just for their potential for career advancement but for their alignment with his personal values and the impact they can have on society. This shift represents a more holistic approach to his work.

Thabo becomes more selective in the projects he undertakes. He seeks out opportunities that resonate with his principles, such as technological innovations that address social issues or initiatives that promote sustainability. This discernment in choosing his work ensures that his efforts are both personally fulfilling and professionally rewarding.

Thabo's interactions with colleagues and clients are now marked by a heightened sense of purpose and authenticity. He engages in conversations and collaborations with a focus on transparency and mutual respect. His approach is to build genuine connections rather than just transactional relationships.

A key aspect of Thabo's renewed approach is his commitment to maintaining integrity and authenticity in all his professional dealings. He upholds his ethical standards and stays true to his values, even when faced with challenging situations or decisions. Thabo also assumes a role in advocating for positive change within the workplace. He champions practices that foster ethical conduct, inclusivity, and a balanced work-life culture. His experiences in the Drakensberg have instilled in him a sense of responsibility to contribute positively to his professional environment.

As the section concludes, Thabo steps into his role with a sense of confidence and centeredness. His clarity about what success means to him and his commitment to his values guide his decisions and interactions. He is ready to navigate the complexities of the professional world with a renewed approach that aligns with his true self. "A Renewed Professional Approach" in "Return to Johannesburg: A Changed Perspective" illustrates how Thabo's personal growth and reflections have translated into a more mindful and value-oriented approach to his career. This section emphasizes the importance of aligning professional endeavours with personal values and the positive impact this alignment can have on both individual fulfilment and broader societal contributions.

As Thabo reintegrates into his professional circle in Johannesburg, his evolved outlook reshapes his interactions with colleagues and peers, leading to a redefinition of his professional relationships. Upon his return, Thabo's colleagues immediately notice a change in his demeanour. The once exclusively goal-driven professional now exudes a more composed and centred aura. His confidence is grounded not in arrogance but in a clear understanding of his values and goals. This transformation intrigues and, in some cases, inspires those around him.

With his new perspective, Thabo reassesses his professional relationships. He now seeks deeper connections based on mutual respect and shared values, rather than purely transactional interactions. He is more mindful of the intentions behind these relationships, choosing to engage more closely with those who demonstrate authenticity and integrity.

Thabo actively works to strengthen relationships with colleagues who share his commitment to ethical practices and meaningful work. He fosters open communication and collaboration, aiming to create a network of professionals united by common goals and ideals. These relationships become a source of mutual support and inspiration.

Conversely, Thabo distances himself from relationships characterized by superficiality or deceit. He tactfully disengages from colleagues who prioritize personal gain over collective success or those who engage in unethical practices. This decision to distance himself is not made out of judgment but from a desire to align his professional life with his personal values. In his quest for more authentic professional relationships, Thabo invests time and effort in nurturing genuine connections. He engages in meaningful conversations, offers support where needed, and seeks to understand the aspirations and challenges of his colleagues, building a foundation of trust and respect.

As this section concludes, Thabo has successfully realigned his professional network to reflect his new insights and values. This redefined network not only supports his professional growth but also contributes to a more fulfilling and authentic work environment. Thabo's approach to relationships demonstrates his belief in the power of collaboration and shared values in achieving collective success and personal fulfilment.

"Navigating Old Relationships with New Insights" in "Return to Johannesburg: A Changed Perspective" highlights Thabo's redefined approach to professional relationships. His experiences lead him to value authenticity and mutual respect, reshaping his interactions and building a network that aligns with his personal and professional values.

.

In the wake of his introspective journey, Thabo understands the vital role of a supportive network in personal and professional growth. This section of the chapter focuses on how he reconnects with key allies and mentors, reinforcing the foundations of his career and personal development. Thabo's time in the Drakensberg brings a newfound appreciation for the mentors and allies who have supported him throughout his career. He recognizes the invaluable role these individuals have played, not just in his professional advancements but also in shaping his character and perspective.

Upon his return, Thabo takes the initiative to reconnect with his mentors. He arranges meetings to express his gratitude and to share his recent experiences and learnings. These meetings are candid and reflective, allowing for a two-way exchange of insights and advice. Thabo also reaches out to professional allies - colleagues and peers who have shown mutual respect and support in the past. He rekindles these relationships, seeking to build on the foundation of trust and collaboration they had established. These renewed connections are marked by a deeper level of understanding and shared vision.

In these reconnections, Thabo finds not only support but also opportunities for mutual growth. Discussions with mentors and allies often lead to collaborative ideas, new projects, and strategies for navigating the complexities of the tech industry. This reciprocal exchange of support and ideas enriches Thabo's professional journey. Thabo's approach to rebuilding his professional network is centred around authenticity and mutual respect. He is more discerning in his interactions, focusing on relationships that offer genuine support and constructive feedback. This network becomes a pillar of strength, offering guidance, encouragement, and a sense of community.

As the section concludes, Thabo stands reinforced by a network of mentors and allies who share his values and aspirations. This support system is not just a professional asset but a source of personal strength and motivation. Thabo's deliberate effort to reconnect with these individuals underscores his recognition of the importance of supportive relationships in achieving both personal fulfilment and professional success. "Reconnecting with Supportive Networks" in "Return to Johannesburg: A Changed Perspective" illustrates Thabo's recognition of the importance of mentorship and supportive relationships. His intentional effort to reconnect and strengthen these bonds reflects his commitment to a career path grounded in shared values, mutual respect, and collaborative growth.

Thabo's transformation, catalysed by his retreat to the Drakensberg, significantly influences how he navigates the corporate landscape. This section of the chapter delves into how he incorporates his newfound insights into his professional life. The challenges that once seemed daunting in the corporate world now appear more manageable to Thabo.

He tackles them with a balanced view, combining his technical expertise with the emotional intelligence and resilience he has developed. This approach allows him to navigate complexities with a calm and strategic mindset.

Thabo's enhanced resilience, forged through his experiences of betrayal and introspection, becomes a key asset in dealing with high-pressure situations. He remains composed under stress, thinks clearly, and makes decisions that are not only effective but also aligned with his values.

With a clearer understanding of his professional goals and personal values, Thabo's decision-making process becomes more strategic. He evaluates opportunities and challenges not just on their surface merits but based on how they align with his long-term objectives and ethical standards.

Thabo becomes an advocate for creating a positive and ethical work environment. He encourages open communication, fosters teamwork, and advocates for policies that support work-life balance and ethical practices. His leadership style evolves to become more inclusive and supportive. Thabo's authentic and value-driven approach earns him the trust and respect of his colleagues and superiors. His credibility in the workplace increases as he consistently demonstrates integrity and competence in his role.

As the section concludes, Thabo establishes himself as a role model in the corporate world. His journey from experiencing betrayal to finding strength and clarity becomes a testament to the power of resilience and introspection. He continues to apply the lessons from the Drakensberg in his daily work, contributing not only to his personal success but also to the betterment of his professional environment. "Applying Lessons in the Corporate World" in "Return to Johannesburg: A Changed Perspective" highlights Thabo's successful integration of personal growth into his professional life. His experiences lead to a more balanced, resilient, and strategic approach in the corporate world, making him a more effective and respected professional.

Thabo's return to the corporate world in Johannesburg is marked by a new approach to his work, deeply influenced by the insights gained during his time in the Drakensberg. This part of the chapter focuses on how he implements these lessons in his day-to-day professional life. In the corporate environment of Johannesburg, Thabo's newly gained perspective from his time in the Drakensberg becomes evident in his approach to tackling challenges. This section of the chapter highlights how he applies a balanced approach to his professional life.

Thabo's decision-making process has evolved to include a careful consideration of both the immediate and the long-term impacts of his actions. Instead of reacting impulsively or focusing solely on short-term gains, he takes the time to analyse how his decisions will affect his projects, his team, and his personal goals in the long run. Faced with high-pressure situations, Thabo remains grounded, keeping the bigger picture in mind. His ability to maintain perspective helps him navigate workplace stress without losing focus on what truly matters. This approach allows him to make more thoughtful and effective decisions.

Complex problems in the workplace, which previously might have provoked anxiety or a rushed response, are now met with a poised and considered approach. Thabo takes the time to understand all facets of a problem, consulting with colleagues and drawing on his experiences to find the best solutions. Thabo's balanced perspective extends beyond his work. He ensures that his professional responsibilities do not overwhelm his personal life. By setting boundaries and managing his time effectively, he maintains a healthy work-life balance, which in turn contributes to his overall effectiveness at work.

In team settings, Thabo encourages a balanced approach to problem-solving. He promotes open discussions where different viewpoints are considered, leading to more collaborative and well-rounded solutions. His emphasis on balance and inclusivity enhances team dynamics and project outcomes.

As this section concludes, Thabo's balanced approach to workplace challenges has not only enhanced his effectiveness as a professional but also positioned him as a leader and role model in his organization. His colleagues appreciate his ability to remain calm and thoughtful under pressure, and his team benefits from his inclusive and strategic approach to problem-solving.

"A Balanced Approach to Challenges" in "Return to Johannesburg: A Changed Perspective" showcases Thabo's growth as a professional who skilfully balances immediate needs with long-term goals. His ability to maintain perspective and poise in the face of complex challenges marks a significant development in his career, reflecting the profound impact of his introspective journey in the Drakensberg.

Thabo's experiences, both personal and professional, have culminated in a heightened level of resilience. This newfound strength is a crucial element in his approach to the challenges and pressures of the corporate world in Johannesburg. In the past, high-pressure situations might have elicited a more anxious response from Thabo. Now, armed with enhanced resilience, he faces these situations with a remarkable calmness. This steadiness not only allows him to think more clearly under pressure but also sets a reassuring tone for his team.

Tight deadlines, a common stressor in the corporate environment, are now navigated by Thabo with greater efficiency and less stress. His ability to remain composed and focused, even when time is of the essence, results in higher quality work and better decision-making. Setbacks and failures, which are inevitable in any professional journey, are now met with a resilient mindset by Thabo.

Instead of dwelling on the disappointment, he quickly assesses what can be learned from the experience and how to move forward. This agility in bouncing back keeps him and his projects on track.

Thabo's resilience contributes significantly to his ability to maintain focus and productivity, even in challenging circumstances. He manages stress more effectively, ensuring that it does not hinder his performance or well-being. Thabo's resilience becomes an inspiration to his colleagues. They notice his ability to handle difficult situations gracefully and start to look up to him as a model of strength and stability. His resilience has a positive ripple effect, encouraging a more resilient culture within his team.

As the section concludes, Thabo stands as a testament to the power of resilience in the corporate world. The challenges he faced have not only strengthened him but also equipped him with the tools to navigate the ups and downs of his career with confidence and grace. His journey from vulnerability to resilience is a key aspect of his professional growth and success.

"Leveraging Enhanced Resilience" in "Return to Johannesburg: A Changed Perspective" highlights how Thabo's personal growth journey has fortified his resilience, profoundly impacting his approach to work. This resilience not only enhances his own performance and well-being but also serves as an inspiration to those around him, fostering a more resilient and supportive work environment.

Thabo's enhanced perspective, shaped by his experiences and reflections, significantly influences his approach to decision-making in the corporate environment. This section of the chapter focuses on how he applies strategic thinking to his professional choices. One of the most notable changes in Thabo's approach is the alignment of his decisions with his personal values and redefined goals. He no longer makes choices based solely on professional advancement or external expectations. Instead, he considers how each decision aligns with his principles and long-term objectives.

Thabo takes a holistic view when evaluating new opportunities. He assesses potential projects not just for their immediate benefits but also for their impact on his personal development, work-life balance, and contribution to society. This comprehensive evaluation helps him choose paths that are fulfilling and meaningful. In his decision-making process, Thabo now places greater emphasis on the long-term consequences of his actions. He thinks several steps ahead, considering the potential ripple effects of his decisions on his career, colleagues, and the wider community.

Thabo recognizes the value of diverse perspectives in strategic decision-making. He actively consults with mentors, peers, and his team, seeking their insights and feedback. This collaborative approach enriches his understanding of different facets of each decision and leads to more well-rounded outcomes.

Another aspect of Thabo's strategic thinking is his approach to risk. He carefully weighs the potential rewards against the risks, making calculated decisions that balance ambition with prudence. This balanced approach to risk helps him navigate the uncertainties of the corporate world with confidence.

As this section concludes, Thabo has established himself as a strategic and visionary leader in his field. His decisions are respected and admired for their depth, foresight, and alignment with his values. This strategic approach has not only enhanced his professional success but also contributed to his sense of fulfilment and purpose in his career. "Strategic Thinking in Decision Making" in "Return to Johannesburg: A Changed Perspective" emphasizes Thabo's growth into a strategic and thoughtful decision-maker. His approach, grounded in personal values and long-term vision, exemplifies how strategic thinking can lead to both professional success and personal fulfilment.

Thabo's renewed approach to his professional life includes a commitment to fostering a positive and supportive work environment. This section of the chapter explores how his leadership style evolves to create a more inclusive and collaborative workplace. One of Thabo's key initiatives is to encourage open communication within his team and the broader organization.

He establishes regular team meetings and feedback sessions where everyone is encouraged to share their ideas and concerns. This open dialogue fosters a culture of transparency and trust, making team members feel valued and heard.

Thabo places a strong emphasis on teamwork and collaborative efforts. He understands that diverse perspectives and skills enhance problem-solving and innovation. By promoting collaboration, he helps break down silos within the organization, leading to more effective and creative solutions.

Understanding the importance of recognition, Thabo makes it a point to acknowledge the contributions and achievements of his colleagues. He celebrates successes, both big and small, and ensures that team members feel appreciated for their efforts. This recognition not only boosts morale but also motivates the team to strive for excellence.

Thabo's leadership style becomes more inclusive. He actively seeks input from all levels of the team and ensures that everyone feels empowered to contribute. He is particularly attentive to including voices that might otherwise be overlooked, fostering a sense of belonging and equity in the workplace.

Thabo advocates for policies and practices that support the well-being of employees. He champions flexible working arrangements, work-life balance, and resources for professional development. His advocacy highlights his understanding that a supportive work environment is key to both employee satisfaction and organizational success.

As the section concludes, Thabo's efforts to nurture a supportive work environment have made a noticeable impact. He has become a catalyst for positive change within the organization, creating a culture where employees feel supported, valued, and motivated. His leadership style, characterized by inclusivity and empathy, sets a new standard in the workplace, contributing to a more engaged and productive team. "Nurturing a Supportive Work Environment" in "Return to Johannesburg: A Changed Perspective" showcases Thabo's role in cultivating a positive and inclusive workplace. His leadership fosters open communication, teamwork, and employee well-being, reflecting his commitment to creating an environment where everyone can thrive and contribute effectively.

Thabo's introspective journey in the Drakensberg Mountains has reinforced his commitment to ethics and integrity, profoundly influencing his approach to his work and interactions in the corporate world. In his day-to-day activities, Thabo places a strong emphasis on ethical practices. He ensures that his decisions and actions in managing projects are guided by principles of honesty, fairness, and responsibility. This approach extends to his interactions with team members, where he fosters a culture of integrity and transparency.

Thabo becomes an active advocate for upholding high ethical standards within his organization. He encourages policies and practices that promote ethical behaviour, such as transparent communication, fair treatment of employees, and responsible handling of data and privacy.

Thabo's unwavering commitment to ethical conduct earns him the trust and respect of both his colleagues and clients. They come to see him as a reliable and principled professional, someone who can be counted on to make the right choices, even in challenging situations.

When faced with ethical dilemmas, Thabo approaches them with careful consideration. He weighs the consequences of various actions, consults with mentors and peers, and opts for solutions that align with his ethical beliefs. His ability to handle such dilemmas with integrity further solidifies his reputation as a morally grounded leader. Thabo's ethical leadership style has a positive influence on his team and peers. He leads by example, inspiring others to also prioritize ethical considerations in their work. This influence helps to foster a work environment where ethical practices are the norm, not the exception.

As the section concludes, Thabo has established himself as a respected leader, known for his ethical practices and principled approach to business. His journey has shown that success and ethics can go hand-in-hand, and that a commitment to integrity can elevate not only one's own career but also the standards of the entire professional community.

"Prioritizing Ethical Practices" in "Return to Johannesburg: A Changed Perspective" underscores Thabo's dedication to maintaining high ethical standards in his professional life. His commitment to integrity and responsible conduct shapes his approach to leadership and decision-making, earning him respect and trust in the corporate world.

The lessons and self-reflection Thabo experienced in the Drakensberg have a profound impact on how he manages the pressures of the corporate world. This part of the chapter highlights his enhanced ability to navigate professional stress with greater ease and effectiveness. Thabo's newfound resilience is most evident in how he maintains his composure in stressful situations. Where he might have previously been prone to anxiety or hasty decisions, he now remains calm and collected. This composure allows him to think more clearly and make sound decisions, even under pressure.

Armed with a clearer mind and a balanced perspective, Thabo tackles challenges with improved problem-solving skills. He approaches problems systematically, considering various angles and potential solutions. His ability to break down complex issues into manageable parts helps in finding effective solutions more efficiently. Thabo's time in the Drakensberg has also helped him cultivate a more positive attitude towards challenges. He views difficulties not as insurmountable obstacles but as opportunities for growth and learning. This positive outlook keeps him motivated and focused, even when facing tough situations.

One significant change in Thabo's approach is his ability to balance his workload effectively. He has learned the importance of delegating tasks, setting realistic deadlines, and taking regular breaks to avoid burnout. This balanced approach to work helps him manage professional pressures without compromising his well-being. Thabo understands the value of seeking support in times of stress. He is more open to discussing challenges with colleagues and superiors and seeking their advice. This willingness to seek help not only alleviates pressure but also fosters a collaborative work environment.

As this section concludes, Thabo's enhanced ability to handle professional pressures is evident. His colleagues and superiors recognize him as a model of resilience in the workplace. Thabo's journey illustrates how personal growth and self-awareness can significantly improve one's ability to manage the demands and stresses of professional life. "Improved Handling of Professional Pressures" in "Return to Johannesburg: A Changed Perspective" demonstrates how Thabo's experiences and self-reflection have equipped him with the skills and mindset to manage workplace stress more effectively. His approach serves as a testament to the importance of personal resilience and a positive attitude in navigating the challenges of the corporate world.

The closing section of this chapter encapsulates Thabo's transformation into a more effective and influential professional, a change driven by his introspective journey and personal growth. Thabo's evolution is recognized not just in his immediate team but across the organization. Colleagues and superiors alike notice the changes in his approach to work and his interactions with others. His leadership style, marked by a combination of resilience, strategic thinking, and ethical practices, garners respect and admiration.

The lessons Thabo has learned and applied in his professional life have significantly enhanced his effectiveness. He navigates complex challenges with ease, communicates more effectively, and inspires his team to perform at their best. His decisions are more impactful, contributing to the success of his projects and the growth of his organization.

Thabo's journey becomes a source of inspiration for others in the workplace. His colleagues are motivated by his ability to balance professional pressures, maintain a positive attitude, and uphold ethical standards. He becomes a role model for how personal development can lead to professional excellence.

Thabo's story highlights the importance of self-reflection and personal growth in one's career. His experiences in the Drakensberg, where he reconnected with his inner self and re-evaluated his priorities, have been pivotal in shaping his professional path. They underscore the idea that taking time to reflect and grow personally can lead to significant improvements in one's professional life.

As Thabo continues his professional journey, he does so with a renewed sense of purpose and clarity. The skills and insights he has gained equip him to face future challenges with confidence. He is committed to continuing his path of personal and professional development, understanding that this journey is ongoing.

Thabo looking ahead to the future, ready to embrace new opportunities and challenges. His transformation into a more effective professional is a testament to the power of personal development and its impact on one's career. Thabo steps into the next chapter of his life with optimism, resilience, and a commitment to excellence.

THE UNMASKING

The Unmasking" is a pivotal chapter in Thabo's story, where he confronts the underlying adversities and deceptions that have been part of his professional journey, leading to a significant turning point in his life.

In this crucial chapter, Thabo takes the bold step of confronting the individuals who had previously undermined his efforts and integrity in the workplace. This decision marks a significant moment in his journey, reflecting his personal growth and desire for resolution. Thabo prepares for these confrontations with a clear mindset. He reflects on what he wants to achieve from these meetings, focusing on expressing his perspective and seeking acknowledgment of the truth, rather than retribution or conflict. He gathers evidence and organizes his thoughts to present his case coherently and objectively.

The most significant of these confrontations is with the colleague who had taken credit for Thabo's work. Thabo approaches this meeting calmly, laying out the facts and expressing how the actions affected him professionally and personally. He seeks acknowledgment of his contribution and an apology, rather than demanding punitive actions. Throughout these meetings, Thabo manages his emotions effectively. While he feels a range of emotions – from disappointment to anger – he remains composed, understanding that losing his temper would only undermine his position and goals.

Thabo's primary goal in these confrontations is to find closure. He wants to put these past adversities behind him so that he can move forward without the burden of unresolved conflicts. These meetings are a step towards that closure, giving him the opportunity to voice his side and clear the air. The reactions Thabo receives vary. While some individuals are defensive, others acknowledge their wrongdoings and offer apologies. Regardless of the outcome, Thabo feels a sense of relief and empowerment for having stood up for himself.

As the section concludes, Thabo emerges from these confrontations with a stronger sense of self. He has confronted his adversaries with dignity and resilience, demonstrating his commitment to honesty and integrity. This experience marks a turning point in his journey, solidifying his resolve to continue his professional path with confidence and self-assuredness.

"Facing Adversaries" in "The Unmasking" is a pivotal section in Thabo's narrative, showcasing his courage and growth as he confronts the challenges of his past. These encounters, while difficult, are essential steps in his journey towards personal and professional fulfilment, marked by his commitment to integrity and closure.

Thabo's confrontations with his adversaries become a platform for revealing the truths obscured by corporate machinations and personal gain. This part of the chapter delves into how he navigates these revelations with a focus on clarity and resolution. Armed with evidence and a clear recollection of events, Thabo systematically presents the facts during each meeting. He lays out timelines, communications, and project details that directly contradict the narratives previously constructed by his adversaries. His presentation is factual and devoid of emotional bias, aimed at revealing the reality of the situations.

More than just presenting facts, Thabo shares his personal perspective on how these events impacted him. He speaks candidly about the feelings of betrayal and frustration he experienced, and how these incidents affected his professional and personal growth. This personal account adds depth and context to the factual narrative. In his interactions, Thabo also tries to understand the motives behind the actions of his adversaries. He asks direct but non-accusatory questions, aiming to uncover the reasons behind their deceitful actions. This approach sheds light on the complexities of human behaviour and the often-grey areas of professional ethics.

Throughout these discussions, Thabo maintains a non-confrontational stance. He is assertive but not aggressive, aiming to foster a dialogue rather than a dispute. His goal is to seek understanding and acknowledgment, not to provoke conflict or defensiveness. The revelations in these meetings have varied impacts. In some cases, they lead to admissions of guilt and apologies; in others, they result in denial and continued resistance. Regardless of the outcome, the act of bringing these truths to light is cathartic and empowering for Thabo.

As the section concludes, Thabo has succeeded in unveiling the hidden truths that marred his professional journey. These revelations, though challenging, have been crucial in his quest for closure and personal growth. The experience reinforces Thabo's commitment to transparency and integrity, and he emerges from these confrontations with a renewed sense of empowerment and clarity.

"Revealing Hidden Truths" in "The Unmasking" is a pivotal part of Thabo's story, highlighting his courage and determination to confront the past and unearth the realities that have impacted his career. This process of revelation is a crucial step in his journey, enabling him to move forward with a deeper understanding and a reaffirmed commitment to his values.

Thabo's confrontations with his adversaries become a defining moment in his narrative, symbolizing not only the resolution of past conflicts but also a significant transformation in his personal and professional life. These meetings allow Thabo to close the chapter on past grievances and misunderstandings. By addressing these issues head-on, he is able to put to rest the lingering effects of the conflicts that had weighed on him. This resolution is a crucial step in moving forward without the burden of unresolved issues.

Thabo's approach to these confrontations reflects his considerable personal growth. He handles potentially volatile situations with a level of maturity and wisdom that was not as evident in his earlier professional life. This growth is a testament to his experiences and the introspection he undertook during his time away.

These events also mark Thabo's maturation as a professional. He transitions from being reactive to proactive, from a position of vulnerability to one of strength. He demonstrates that he can navigate the complexities of the corporate world with a balanced approach, maintaining his principles while effectively addressing challenges.

As a result of how he handles these confrontations, Thabo gains newfound respect from his colleagues and superiors. They recognize his integrity, resilience, and ability to manage difficult situations with grace. This recognition further solidifies his standing in the professional community. Thabo's actions reinforce his commitment to integrity and courage in his professional dealings. He shows that it is possible to confront challenges without compromising ethical standards, setting an example for others in the corporate world.

Thabo looking towards the future with a renewed sense of purpose and confidence. He has navigated a critical turning point in his life, emerging stronger and more focused. Ready to embrace new opportunities and challenges, Thabo steps into the next phase of his career, equipped with the lessons learned and the strength gained from his experiences. "A Major Turning Point" in "The Unmasking" marks a pivotal moment in Thabo's story, signifying his growth and transformation. These confrontations not only resolve past conflicts but also showcase his development into a more mature, resilient, and principled professional. This turning point paves the way for new beginnings in Thabo's career and personal life.

As Thabo navigates through the challenging confrontations with his past adversaries, each encounter brings its own set of outcomes and learnings, contributing significantly to his personal and professional development. Through these confrontations, Thabo gains deeper insights into the nature of trust and professional relationships. He learns to be more discerning about whom to trust and how to build relationships based on mutual respect and shared values. This understanding helps him forge stronger, more authentic connections in his professional life.

Each meeting tests and ultimately strengthens Thabo's resilience. He confronts situations that would have once overwhelmed him, and through these experiences, he builds an even greater capacity to handle adversity. This enhanced resilience becomes a key trait that aids him in future professional challenges. Thabo's journey underscores the importance of standing up for oneself. He realizes that self-advocacy is crucial in the corporate world – not only in addressing wrongs but also in ensuring that one's contributions are recognized and valued. This realization empowers him to be more assertive in future interactions.

Each confrontation, regardless of the outcome, provides valuable lessons. Thabo learns to approach conflict with a balance of firmness and diplomacy. He understands that conflict, when handled constructively, can lead to growth and positive change. These experiences significantly shape Thabo's future approach to his career. He becomes more proactive in addressing issues, more strategic in his decision-making, and more committed to ethical and transparent practices. These changes not only make him a more effective professional but also enrich his personal growth.

As the section concludes, Thabo emerges as a more complete professional, with a well-rounded understanding of the complexities of the corporate world. He has grown not just in his capacity to handle challenges but also in his understanding of human dynamics, ethics, and leadership. This growth positions him well for the next stages of his career and personal journey. "Personal and Professional Growth" in "The Unmasking" highlights the transformative impact of Thabo's confrontations on his development. These experiences, while challenging, serve as catalysts for his growth, equipping him with crucial skills and insights that enrich his professional and personal life.

The Unmasking" represents a pivotal moment in Thabo's narrative, as he transitions into a new phase of his life and career with newfound clarity and self-awareness. Thabo's confrontations and experiences have given him a more nuanced understanding of the corporate world. He now sees it not just as a competitive landscape but as an environment where integrity, resilience, and honesty are equally important for success. This understanding allows him to navigate his professional life with greater wisdom and effectiveness.

The process of facing his adversaries and revealing hidden truths has been akin to unmasking the deeper realities of his work environment. Thabo has learned about the undercurrents of corporate politics, the complexities of human relationships, and the importance of ethical conduct. These revelations have been instrumental in shaping his approach to his career. Through these challenges, Thabo's true strength and character have come to the forefront. He has shown himself to be not only a skilled professional but also a person of integrity and resilience. These qualities have earned him respect and admiration from his peers and have cemented his reputation as a principled leader.

As Thabo concludes this chapter of his journey, he does so with a renewed sense of confidence and direction. He is more certain of his values, his goals, and his approach to achieving them. This confidence is not born out of naivety but out of a deep understanding of himself and the professional world he inhabits.

Equipped with the lessons learned and the growth experienced, Thabo is prepared to face future challenges and opportunities. He steps into the next phase of his career ready to apply his insights, to lead with integrity, and to continue his path of personal and professional development.

Thabo looking forward to the future, ready to embrace the opportunities and challenges that await. He steps into this new light with a clear vision and a strong sense of self, poised to make a positive and meaningful impact in his professional and personal life. The Unmasking" marks a significant turning point in Thabo's journey, symbolizing his transition into a phase of greater clarity, strength, and preparedness. This chapter encapsulates his journey of confronting and overcoming challenges, leading to a profound personal and professional transformation.

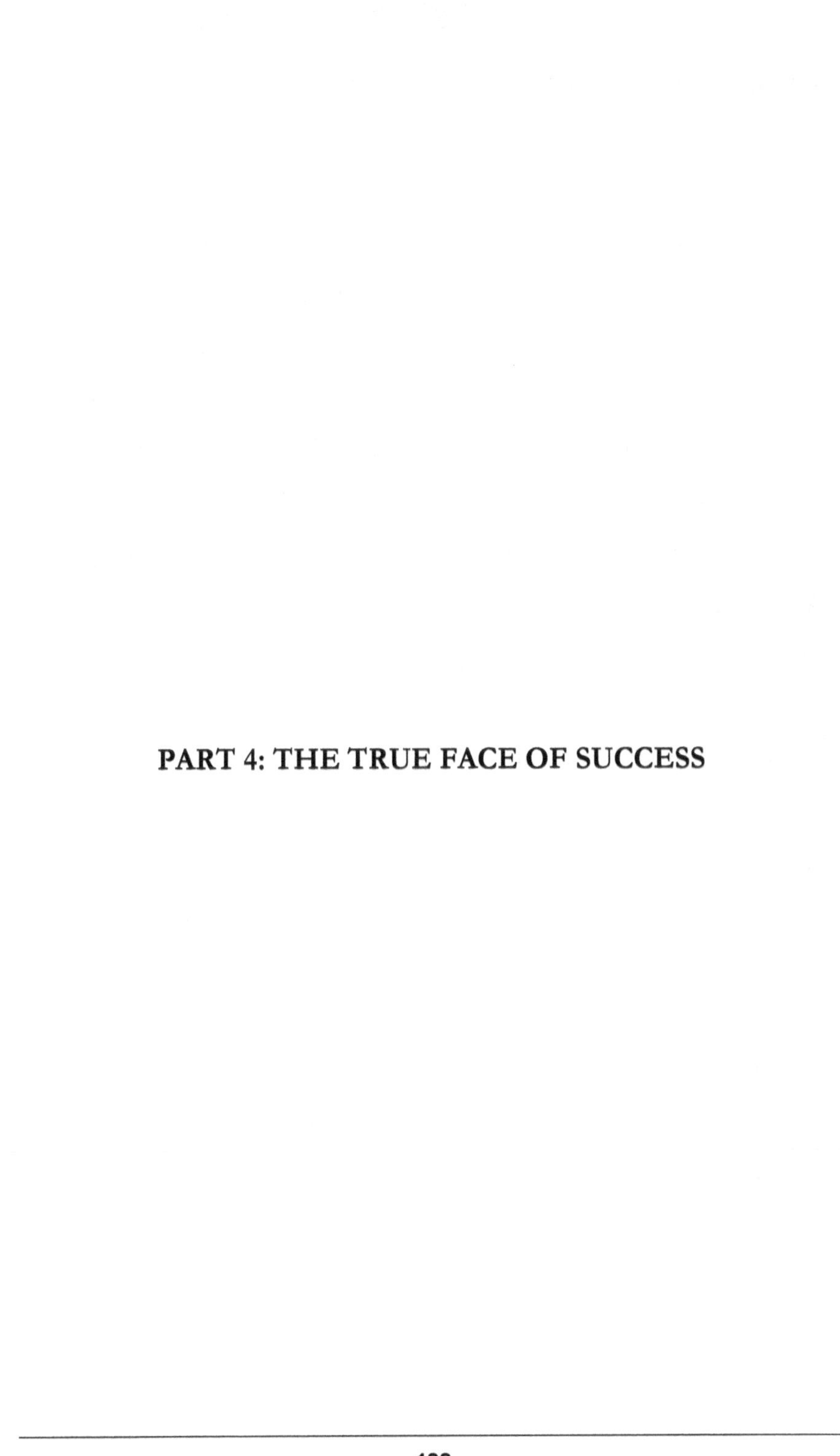

PART 4: THE TRUE FACE OF SUCCESS

REBUILDING AMONGST THE RUINS

In "Rebuilding Amongst the Ruins," Thabo embarks on a journey of renewal and growth, piecing together the fragments of his past experiences to build a more fulfilling and authentic future. Thabo's journey of redefining his professional path, grounded in the lessons he has learned from his past experiences. Thabo takes time to reflect on the challenges he has faced - the betrayals, setbacks, and conflicts. Instead of viewing these experiences negatively, he sees them as valuable lessons that have shaped his resilience and understanding. He acknowledges that these experiences, while difficult, have been instrumental in his personal and professional growth.

With a sense of renewed purpose, Thabo embraces the opportunity to start anew. He approaches this fresh start not with bitterness, but with a sense of optimism and humility. He recognizes that the past cannot be changed, but the future is a blank canvas, ready to be painted with the wisdom of his experiences. The lessons Thabo has learned are now the cornerstones of his approach to his career. He is more discerning in his choices, more strategic in his thinking, and more empathetic in his interactions. These lessons become his guideposts, helping him navigate the complexities of the corporate world with a newfound confidence.

Thabo understands that the foundation for his future success is built on the ruins of his past challenges. He utilizes the strength and resilience he has gained to build a more robust and fulfilling career path. This foundation is not just professional but also personal, as he integrates his values and ethics into his work. As he steps into this new phase, Thabo balances humility with determination. He remains open to learning and growth, acknowledging that he does not have all the answers. At the same time, he is determined to apply what he has learned, to make the most of the opportunities that lie ahead.

Thabo stands poised to embrace the new opportunities that await him. He steps into the future with a clear vision and a resilient spirit, ready to tackle the challenges and seize the opportunities that come his way, armed with the invaluable lessons from his past. "Starting Anew with Lessons Learned" in "Rebuilding Amongst the Ruins" paints a picture of Thabo's readiness to embark on a new chapter in his life. This section highlights how the challenges he has faced have not only fortified him but also provided a deeper insight into navigating his professional journey with greater wisdom and resilience.

In this transformative phase of his life, Thabo adopts a new outlook that reshapes his approach to both his career and personal aspirations. Thabo's definition of success undergoes a significant shift. No longer confined to traditional corporate milestones like promotions or high-profile projects, his idea of success now encompasses personal fulfilment, ethical impact, and meaningful contributions to his field.

This redefinition guides his choices and goals moving forward. Driven by a desire to make a real difference, Thabo looks for work that not only challenges him professionally but also aligns with his personal values. He is drawn to projects that have a positive impact on society, that innovate responsibly, and that contribute to sustainable development.

In his professional interactions, Thabo prioritizes authenticity and mutual respect. He invests time and effort in building genuine relationships with colleagues, mentors, and industry peers. These connections are not merely networking tools; they are partnerships based on shared values and goals.

Thabo's fresh perspective involves integrating his personal values into his professional life. He believes in working with integrity, promoting transparency, and advocating for fairness and inclusivity. This integration creates a sense of harmony and authenticity in his approach to work.

Alongside his professional endeavours, Thabo also focuses on activities and hobbies that bring him personal joy and fulfilment. He understands the importance of a well-rounded life, where personal interests and passions have a place alongside professional commitments.

As the section concludes, Thabo has successfully navigated his way to a renewed professional identity. This new perspective on his career and personal life, rooted in meaningful work and genuine connections, positions him for a future that promises not just success in the traditional sense but fulfilment and purpose. "Embracing a Fresh Perspective" in "Rebuilding Amongst the Ruins" highlights Thabo's evolved approach to his career and personal life. This new outlook, cantered on meaningful work and authentic connections, demonstrates his commitment to a fulfilling and value-driven path.

Thabo's journey leads him to prioritize the cultivation of authentic and meaningful relationships in his professional life, emphasizing the value of true connection and collaboration. Thabo actively reaches out to colleagues, mentors, and industry peers with a renewed sense of openness and honesty. He shares his experiences and learnings, inviting dialogue and exchange. This transparency creates a foundation of trust and mutual respect in his relationships.

In forging new connections, Thabo seeks individuals and organizations that share his values and vision. He looks for partners who are committed to ethical practices, innovation with a purpose, and fostering positive change. These shared values become the bedrock of these newly formed relationships. Thabo emphasizes collaborative growth in his interactions.

He engages in projects and discussions where both parties can learn from each other, contribute to mutual goals, and grow together. He sees each relationship as an opportunity for shared development, rather than just a means to an end.

Gone are the days of superficial networking for Thabo. He approaches networking with a purpose, seeking connections that are not just professionally advantageous but also personally enriching. He values quality over quantity in his professional network. Recognizing the value of mentorship in his own journey, Thabo also becomes a mentor to others. He shares his experiences and insights, guiding and supporting others in their professional paths. This role of mentorship is a reflection of his commitment to giving back and fostering a culture of learning and support.

As this section concludes, Thabo has built a network characterized by authenticity, mutual respect, and collaborative growth. These genuine connections not only enrich his professional life but also contribute to his personal fulfilment. Thabo's approach to relationships demonstrates his belief in the power of true connection and collaboration in achieving both personal satisfaction and professional success.

"Forming Genuine Connections" in "Rebuilding Amongst the Ruins" illustrates Thabo's intentional effort to build meaningful professional relationships. This focus on authenticity, shared values, and collaborative growth marks a significant shift in his approach to networking and partnership, reflecting his growth as a person and a professional.

In this next phase of his career, Thabo actively seeks and cultivates partnerships that align with his renewed vision and values, emphasizing collaboration, ethical practices, and meaningful impact. Thabo's approach to forming new partnerships is guided by a desire to connect with individuals and organizations that share his commitment to ethical practices and positive impact. He seeks out those who are not just successful in the conventional sense but are also conscious of their role in society and the industry.

The partnerships Thabo forms are based on mutual goals and visions for change. Whether it's a project that addresses a social issue, a venture that promotes sustainability, or an initiative that drives innovation in ethical ways, each partnership is chosen for its potential to create meaningful impact. Thabo approaches these partnerships with the aim of mutual growth. He believes in the power of collaboration where all parties can learn, develop, and benefit. This approach fosters an environment of shared knowledge and skills, leading to more robust and innovative outcomes. For Thabo, these new partnerships transcend traditional business transactions. They are relationships built on a foundation of trust, respect, and a shared desire to contribute positively to the world. He views these partnerships as long-term collaborations that go beyond mere profit-making.

In building these partnerships, Thabo values and integrates diverse perspectives and ideas. He understands that diversity in thought and experience leads to more comprehensive and effective solutions. This openness to different viewpoints is a key aspect of his collaborative approach.

As the section concludes, Thabo has established a network of partnerships that reflect his personal and professional evolution. These partnerships are not just strategic alliances but are relationships that embody his values and vision. Through these collaborations, Thabo not only contributes to his personal and professional growth but also impacts the industry and society positively. Thabo's commitment to establishing collaborative and ethical partnerships. These alliances are a reflection of his values and his desire to effect positive change, demonstrating his belief in the power of collective effort and integrity in professional endeavours.

Thabo's transformation extends to his approach to leadership, where he embraces a style that is empathetic, inclusive, and focused on nurturing the growth of others. This evolution in his leadership approach marks a significant shift in how he influences and guides his team and organization. Thabo's leadership is now deeply rooted in empathy. He makes efforts to understand the perspectives, challenges, and motivations of his team members. This empathetic approach helps him connect with his team on a more personal level, fostering a trusting and open work environment.

Inclusivity becomes a cornerstone of Thabo's leadership style. He ensures that all voices are heard and valued, creating a space where diverse ideas and perspectives are welcomed and encouraged. This inclusive approach leads to richer discussions, more innovative solutions, and a stronger sense of belonging among team members.

Thabo is committed to nurturing the potential of his colleagues and team members. He invests time in mentoring and supporting their professional development, recognizing and cultivating their strengths, and providing opportunities for them to grow and excel.

Through his leadership, Thabo inspires a culture of support and collaboration within the organization. He leads by example, showing that success is not just about individual achievement but about working together and supporting each other. This approach fosters a more cohesive and motivated team. Thabo's leadership style is adaptive; he recognizes that different situations and individuals may require different approaches.

He remains flexible and responsive to the changing needs of his team and the organization, ensuring that his leadership remains effective and relevant. Thabo has become a respected and inspirational leader in his organization. His approach to leadership, characterized by empathy, inclusivity, and a focus on nurturing others, has not only enhanced the performance and morale of his team but has also contributed to a more positive and collaborative organizational culture.

Thabo's journey, as he stands on the threshold of a new chapter in his life, ready to apply the lessons and insights he has gained. The chapter ends with Thabo poised at the beginning of a new era in his career. He has navigated through a period of significant upheaval and emerged with a clearer vision for his future.

The challenges he faced have not defeated him; instead, they have provided him with a foundation of strength and wisdom on which to build his future endeavours. Thabo's experiences, symbolized by the metaphorical ruins around him, have imparted valuable lessons. These lessons include the importance of integrity in the workplace, the power of resilience, and the value of authentic relationships. He views these ruins not as remnants of failure but as stepping stones to greater achievements.

Looking forward, Thabo is filled with a sense of anticipation and optimism. He recognizes that the path ahead will have its challenges, but he feels equipped to face them with the knowledge and skills he has acquired. He is ready to embrace new opportunities and continue his journey of personal and professional growth. Thabo's renewed sense of purpose drives him as he steps into the future. He is committed to applying his learnings in a way that not only advances his career but also contributes positively to those around him and to the broader industry.

Thabo looking towards the horizon with hope and optimism. He is no longer the same person who faced those challenges; he has grown, evolved, and is now ready to embark on this next phase of his life with a renewed sense of purpose and a positive outlook. As "Rebuilding Amongst the Ruins" concludes, Thabo stands ready to embark on a new journey, one that is informed by his past but not defined by it. He steps forward with the confidence of someone who has faced adversity and emerged stronger, ready to explore what the future holds with enthusiasm and optimism.

Thabo's resilience and growth. He has transformed challenges into opportunities for learning and development, laying a strong foundation for the next phase of his journey. Thabo's narrative, one that sets the stage for continued growth and success.

Thabo embarks on an exciting new venture in Cape Town, a project that marks a significant shift in his professional journey and embodies his new approach to success. The chapter begins with Thabo unveiling his new project in Cape Town. This initiative represents a fusion of cutting-edge technology with a strong social impact focus.

The project aims to leverage technological innovation to address key societal challenges, making it a venture that resonates deeply with Thabo's values and vision. The project holds a special significance for Thabo, as it aligns closely with his personal beliefs and the lessons he has learned throughout his journey. It's a culmination of his experiences, embodying his commitment to making a difference through his work.

Thabo's project is ambitious, targeting not just commercial success but also aiming to create a lasting positive impact in the community. The goals of the project are twofold: to establish a successful, sustainable business model and to bring about tangible social change in Cape Town.

At the heart of the project is the integration of technology and social good. Thabo and his team are working on innovative solutions that can help solve local problems, such as improving access to education, enhancing healthcare services, or supporting sustainable practices in the community. From the outset, Thabo involves various stakeholders in the project. He engages with community leaders, potential users, and industry experts to ensure that the project's direction is informed, relevant, and sustainable. This inclusive approach is central to the project's ethos.

As the project progresses, Thabo encounters various challenges, from logistical hurdles to funding issues. However, his new perspective allows him to navigate these challenges differently. He approaches each obstacle with resilience, creativity, and an unwavering focus on the project's core objectives. The section concludes with the project successfully taking off, generating interest and support from various quarters. While it's still early days, the initial success and positive reception of the project validate Thabo's vision and approach.

He stands at the helm of this venture, not just as a business leader but as a champion of technology's role in societal betterment.
"Launching the New Project" in "A New Vision in Cape Town" marks the beginning of an exciting and meaningful chapter in Thabo's career.

This project, blending technology and social impact, embodies his commitment to creating work that is not only commercially viable but also socially responsible and impactful. In this pivotal chapter, Thabo demonstrates a transformative approach to success, reshaping his goals and aspirations to encompass not just professional achievement but also meaningful social impact.

Thabo's perspective on what constitutes success undergoes a profound change. No longer confined to financial gains and corporate accolades, his definition of success expands to include the positive impact his work can have on society. This shift reflects a maturation in his professional outlook, where the value of work is measured by its contribution to the greater good.

The objectives of Thabo's new project in Cape Town are cantered around creating a tangible, positive impact in the community. He is motivated by the potential to effect change, whether it's through technological innovation, social improvement, or environmental sustainability. His goals are ambitious but deeply rooted in a desire to make a difference.

Thabo's approach to the project takes a holistic view of achievement. He considers the success of the venture not just in terms of profit margins but also in its ability to meet the needs of the community, to be sustainable over the long term, and to align with ethical practices. In this new phase of his career, Thabo prioritizes purpose over profit. While financial sustainability remains important, it is no longer the sole driver of his decisions. He is willing to explore paths that might be less lucrative in the short term if they promise greater societal benefit.

Success in Thabo's project is also gauged by its real-world impact. Metrics of success include the number of people positively affected, the extent of societal problems addressed, and the sustainability of the solutions provided. Thabo establishes systems to measure and evaluate these impact metrics regularly. Thabo's new vision of success represents a significant departure from traditional business metrics. He is embarking on a path where success is interwoven with social responsibility and positive impact. This approach not only makes his work more fulfilling but also sets a new standard for what it means to be successful in the modern corporate world.

Thabo's evolved understanding of success, where impact and purpose are as important as profitability and growth. This shift in perspective signifies a deeper alignment of his professional goals with his personal values, setting a new paradigm for success in the business world. In the development of his ambitious project in Cape Town, Thabo leverages the valuable lessons learned from his past experiences, incorporating them into every aspect of the project to ensure its success and integrity.

Thabo's past experiences have honed his resilience, which he now applies to overcoming challenges in the project. Whether navigating logistical hurdles, managing resource constraints, or addressing unforeseen obstacles, he remains steadfast and resourceful, viewing each challenge as an opportunity for growth and innovation.

Drawing on his evolved leadership skills, Thabo fosters an inclusive and empathetic team environment. He actively listens to his team members, values their contributions, and ensures that everyone feels respected and involved. This inclusive approach enhances team cohesion and drives better collaboration and creativity. Ethical practices are at the forefront of Thabo's project management approach. He ensures transparency in operations, fairness in decision-making, and accountability at all levels. His commitment to ethics not only builds trust within the team and with stakeholders but also aligns the project with his personal values.

Thabo recognizes the importance of stakeholder feedback and incorporates this into the project's development process. He engages with community members, industry experts, and potential users to gather insights and perspectives, using this feedback to refine and improve the project.

Thabo's past experiences have taught him to balance his vision with practical considerations. While he is ambitious and forward-thinking, he also remains grounded in reality, ensuring that the project's goals are achievable and sustainable.

Thabo's journey, shaped significantly by the lessons he has learned along the way. His approach reflects a blend of ambition, resilience, empathy, and ethical commitment, setting the project on a course for success that is both impactful and sustainable. A New Vision in Cape Town" highlights how Thabo's past challenges and learnings have become instrumental in shaping his approach to his new project. By applying these lessons, he not only enhances the project's chances for success but also ensures that it reflects his values and commitment to making a positive difference.

Thabo places a strong emphasis on building a collaborative team, recognizing that a diverse and cohesive group is essential to the success of his project in Cape Town. Thabo carefully selects a team of professionals from various backgrounds and expertise. He understands that diversity in skills, experiences, and perspectives can drive innovation and creativity. Each team member is chosen not only for their professional abilities but also for their alignment with the project's vision and values.

One of Thabo's priorities is to foster a culture where open communication is the norm. He encourages team members to share their ideas and opinions freely, ensuring that everyone feels heard and valued. Regular team meetings and brainstorming sessions become a platform for this exchange of ideas.

Respect and inclusivity are key tenets of Thabo's team culture. He promotes an environment where differences are respected and valued, and where each team member feels included and integral to the project's success. This approach strengthens team cohesion and morale.

In this collaborative setting, Thabo encourages his team to think outside the box and to approach problems with creative solutions. He supports risk-taking and experimentation, understanding that innovation often requires stepping out of comfort zones. Thabo empowers his team members by entrusting them with responsibilities and valuing their contributions. He provides the resources and support needed for them to excel in their roles, helping them to develop professionally and personally.

As the section concludes, Thabo's team has evolved into a dynamic and cohesive unit. The collaborative atmosphere he has fostered leads to a synergistic work environment where the collective effort is greater than the sum of its parts.

The team is not only working towards the successful completion of the project but also embodying the principles of teamwork, innovation, and mutual respect.

Thabo's commitment to creating a team environment that is diverse, open, and innovative. His leadership fosters a collaborative culture that is crucial to the project's success, emphasizing the value of each team member's contribution and creating a space where creativity and innovation can thrive.

Thabo's project in Cape Town is characterized by a strong emphasis on sustainability, reflecting his commitment to creating a positive and lasting impact on both the environment and the community. Thabo ensures that the project's business model is sustainable over the long term. This involves careful planning for financial viability without compromising ethical standards or environmental responsibilities. He seeks to create a model that balances profitability with social and environmental welfare.

A significant aspect of the project's sustainability focus is on minimizing its environmental impact. Thabo and his team incorporate eco-friendly practices and technologies, aiming to reduce carbon footprints, manage waste efficiently, and utilize renewable energy sources wherever possible.

Understanding the importance of the project's impact on the local community, Thabo engages with community leaders and members to ensure that the project addresses their needs and contributes positively to their well-being. He views the community as a key stakeholder in the project, seeking their input and ensuring that the benefits of the project are shared.

Thabo is committed to maintaining ethical and responsible practices throughout the project. This includes fair labour practices, responsible sourcing of materials, and transparency in operations. He believes that ethical business is not just a duty but a cornerstone of long-term success.

Part of the project's sustainability focus involves educating team members, stakeholders, and the community about environmental and social responsibility. Thabo initiates programs and workshops to raise awareness and promote sustainable practices within and beyond the project.

As the section concludes, Thabo's project stands as a model for sustainable business practices. The emphasis on environmental sustainability, community engagement, and ethical practices demonstrates his vision of a responsible business that creates value not just economically, but also socially and environmentally.

Thabo's dedication to integrating sustainability into every facet of his project. His approach highlights the importance of responsible business practices that encompass environmental stewardship, community well-being, and ethical operations, setting a precedent for future business endeavours.

Thabo's project takes a community-centric approach, actively engaging with the people of Cape Town to ensure that the project not only benefits from local insights but also contributes positively to the community. From the outset, Thabo prioritizes engagement with the Cape Town community. He understands that for the project to be truly successful and impactful, it must resonate with and meet the needs of the local population. This engagement is not an afterthought but a fundamental aspect of the project's planning and execution.

Thabo reaches out to local leaders, community organizations, and advocacy groups to gather insights and gain a deeper understanding of the community's needs and challenges. These collaborations are based on mutual respect and a shared goal of uplifting the community. In decision-making processes, Thabo ensures that the voices of the community members are heard and considered. He sets up forums and meetings where community members can provide input, express concerns, and offer suggestions. This inclusive approach helps tailor the project to be more effective and beneficial for the community.

The project is designed to provide tangible benefits to the community, such as job creation, skill development, and improved access to services or technology. Thabo actively involves community members in various phases of the project, fostering a sense of ownership and partnership. Thabo and his team work on addressing issues that are specific to the Cape Town community. This may include initiatives focused on education, healthcare, environmental conservation, or economic development, depending on the community's needs and the project's scope.

Thabo's project has become a beacon of community-driven development. The active engagement with the Cape Town community ensures that the project is not only viable and sustainable but also deeply rooted in the local context, addressing real needs and contributing to the community's well-being.

Thabo's commitment to creating a project that is deeply integrated with and beneficial to the local community. His approach emphasizes the importance of community involvement and collaboration, ensuring that the project's impact is both meaningful and sustainable.

Thabo's innovative project, reflecting his evolved perspective on success and his commitment to making a difference. Thabo's project is showing early signs of success. The groundwork laid in terms of community engagement, sustainable practices, and a collaborative team effort is paying off.

The project is not only meeting its initial targets but also making a positive impact in the Cape Town community. Thabo's project transcends the traditional boundaries of a business venture. It embodies his commitment to integrating social responsibility, ethical integrity, and sustainability into the fabric of his work. This project is a reflection of his belief that business can and should be a force for good.

The progress of the project is a tangible manifestation of Thabo's new vision for success. This vision, which balances professional achievements with a deep commitment to societal and environmental well-being, is coming to life through the project's development and impact.

Thabo's approach to this project serves as a model for how businesses can operate with a conscience. It demonstrates how integrating ethical practices, community involvement, and environmental considerations can lead to a successful, sustainable, and socially responsible business. While the project is still in its early stages, the positive beginnings are a source of motivation for Thabo and his team. They are inspired to continue pushing boundaries, innovating, and striving for impact, knowing that their efforts are contributing to a greater cause.

Thabo looking forward to the future of the project with optimism and determination. He is poised to continue leading the project towards greater heights, guided by a vision that aligns his professional aspirations with his values and commitment to making a meaningful difference in the world. Thabo's journey, where his aspirations for creating a business that is both successful and socially responsible are beginning to materialize. This chapter encapsulates the essence of Thabo's new approach to success, one that is deeply rooted in ethical integrity, social responsibility, and a commitment to positive change.

Thabo's journey, marking a personal and professional triumph that underscores the enduring value of resilience and integrity in his life. Thabo marks a significant achievement in his Cape Town project, a milestone that resonates deeply with his personal and professional growth.

Thabo and his team celebrate the successful launch of a key phase of their Cape Town project. This moment is more than just a professional victory; it's a symbol of the journey Thabo has undertaken, reflecting the sweat, dedication, and innovation that have gone into making this project a reality.

As Thabo stands amidst the celebration, he reflects on his personal journey. This milestone encapsulates the challenges he has overcome, the risks he has taken, and the perseverance he has shown. It's a testament to his resilience and his commitment to making a positive impact through his work.

The success of the project is the result of Thabo's relentless hard work and his willingness to think outside the box. He has pushed boundaries, introduced innovative solutions, and led his team through uncharted territories to achieve this remarkable feat.

Throughout the project, Thabo has remained steadfast in his values and integrity. This victory is not just about achieving a goal but also about how it was achieved. It stands as proof that success can be attained without compromising on ethics and principles. This moment of victory is emblematic of Thabo's resilience. Through every setback and challenge, he has remained committed to his vision, demonstrating that resilience is not just about enduring but also about thriving and innovating in the face of adversity.

As the celebration continues, Thabo takes a moment to acknowledge and thank his team, recognizing that this achievement is the fruit of collective effort. There is a sense of shared pride and accomplishment, and a deep appreciation for the journey that has led them to this point.

The Celebration of Resilience is not just a celebration of a project's success but a poignant acknowledgment of Thabo's personal and professional growth. It highlights the journey of hard work, innovation, and unwavering dedication to values that have culminated in this significant achievement.

Thabo's journey, underscoring how his ability to endure and flourish through adversity has been fundamental to his success. As Thabo and his team celebrate their achievement, there is a profound recognition of the resilience that has been pivotal to reaching this point. This celebration is not just about the project's success; it's a tribute to the enduring spirit, adaptability, and determination that Thabo has exhibited throughout his journey.

Thabo's path to this moment has been marked by numerous challenges and setbacks. Each obstacle presented an opportunity for growth and learning. His resilience in these moments – choosing to move forward, to find solutions, and to learn from each experience – has been key to his and the project's success.

This victory is a testament to the power of persistence. Thabo's journey demonstrates that enduring through difficult times, staying focused on one's goals, and maintaining a steadfast commitment can lead to remarkable outcomes. His persistence in the face of adversity has not only driven the project forward but also inspired those around him. Thabo's resilience is also characterized by his ability to adapt and grow. Each challenge has contributed to his personal and professional development, equipping him with new skills, insights, and perspectives. This adaptability has been crucial in navigating the complex landscape of his project.

The celebration highlights Thabo's inner strength. His resilience is rooted in a deep sense of self-belief and commitment to his values. It's this inner strength that has enabled him to overcome obstacles and pursue his vision with unwavering dedication. As the section concludes, the significance of resilience in Thabo's story is clear. The celebration is as much an acknowledgment of his resilience as it is of the project's achievement.

It's a powerful reminder that resilience is not just about enduring tough times but about using those experiences to build a path to success. It's a celebration of his tenacity and adaptability, illustrating how these qualities have been instrumental in overcoming challenges and achieving success. This section serves as an inspiring testament to the power of resilience in personal and professional growth.

Thabo's project success serves as a poignant reminder of how his unwavering commitment to integrity has been a guiding force throughout his journey. During the celebration, there is a collective acknowledgment of the crucial role integrity has played in both the project's success and Thabo's personal growth. His commitment to maintaining ethical standards in every aspect of the project has set a strong foundation for its development and success. Thabo's insistence on ethical practices and transparency in all dealings has not only shaped the project's course but also built a culture of trust within his team and with stakeholders.

This dedication to doing the right thing, even in challenging situations, has earned him respect and admiration. Throughout the project, Thabo faced numerous decisions where he had to balance commercial interests with ethical considerations. His choices, consistently rooted in integrity, demonstrated that ethical decision-making is not only the right approach but also beneficial in the long run.

Thabo's unwavering integrity has solidified his reputation as a leader and a visionary in his field. Colleagues, team members, and industry peers view him as a role model for how to lead with principles. His leadership style has inspired others to uphold similar standards of honesty and ethical conduct.

The celebration underscores the notion that true success is not just about achieving goals but also about how those goals are achieved. Thabo's integrity-driven approach has contributed significantly to the project's success, proving that ethical business practices and commercial success are not mutually exclusive. As the section concludes, Thabo's commitment to integrity stands out as a key element of his legacy.

The celebration is not just for a job well done but also for the ethical and transparent manner in which it was accomplished. Thabo's journey exemplifies the idea that integrity and moral leadership are invaluable assets in any successful endeavour.

The Celebration of Resilience" highlights the fundamental role that integrity has played in Thabo's journey. This chapter reinforces the idea that adhering to ethical principles and transparent practices is crucial for long-term success and for building a legacy as a principled leader.

Thabo takes the opportunity during the celebration to reflect on the journey and express his gratitude to those who have been instrumental in the project's success and his personal growth.
Amidst the celebration, Thabo takes a moment to reflect on the path that led to this point. He thinks about the challenges faced, the obstacles overcome, and the milestones achieved.

This reflection deepens his appreciation for the journey and the growth it has entailed, both for the project and for himself personally. Thabo recognizes that the project's success is a result of the collective effort of his dedicated team. He takes the time to personally thank each team member, acknowledging their hard work, commitment, and the unique skills they brought to the project. He emphasizes that each contribution, big or small, was vital to the project's success.

Thabo also extends his gratitude to his mentors and advisors who have guided him through his journey. Their wisdom, support, and encouragement have been invaluable, and he acknowledges their role in shaping his approach and decisions throughout the project.
Understanding the crucial role played by the Cape Town community,

Thabo expresses his gratitude for their support, insights, and participation. He highlights how their involvement enriched the project, ensuring it remained grounded in the community's needs and aspirations.

Thabo emphasizes that the success being celebrated is not just his but shared with everyone who contributed to the project. He speaks about the shared values that united them – a commitment to making a positive impact, fostering sustainability, and upholding integrity. As this section concludes, the celebration becomes an embodiment of shared triumph and mutual gratitude.

Thabo's reflection and acknowledgment of each contributor reinforce the sense of collective achievement and the power of collaboration. It's a testament to the idea that success is most meaningful when it is shared and when it reflects the contributions of a diverse group united by common goals.

 The Celebration of Resilience" underscores the importance of recognizing the collective effort and shared values that underpin successful endeavours. Thabo's acknowledgment of his team, mentors, and community not only highlights the collaborative nature of the project but also reinforces the significance of gratitude and shared success in professional and personal growth.

Thabo's journey and the celebration of his project's success serve as a source of inspiration, influencing his colleagues, peers, and the next generation of professionals and entrepreneurs.

Thabo's story, marked by its highs and lows, resilience, and adherence to integrity, resonates strongly with those around him. His journey serves as a powerful example of how challenges can be navigated with perseverance and ethical conduct, inspiring others to follow a similar path.

Through his actions and achievements, Thabo becomes a role model, particularly for aspiring entrepreneurs and professionals. They look up to him not just for his professional success but for the manner in which he has achieved it.

His commitment to his values and principles, even in the face of adversity, sets a standard for others to emulate. Thabo's success story encourages others to consider ethical entrepreneurship as a viable and rewarding path. He demonstrates that it is possible to build a successful business while also contributing positively to society and staying true to one's values. As part of the celebration, Thabo shares the lessons he has learned throughout his journey.

His insights on resilience, integrity, and the importance of community engagement are particularly impactful for those looking to make their mark in the business world.

Thabo's approach and success motivate a change in the industry's perspective on success. His peers and competitors begin to see the value in approaches that prioritize sustainability, community involvement, and ethical practices, leading to a gradual shift in business practices.

As the section concludes, Thabo stands not just as a successful entrepreneur but as a beacon of hope and integrity. His journey and the celebration of his success inspire a new wave of professionals and entrepreneurs who aspire to achieve success while upholding their values and making a positive impact on the world.

The Celebration of Resilience" highlights Thabo's influence beyond the confines of his project, extending to his peers, colleagues, and future entrepreneurs. His story becomes a source of motivation and a testament to the possibility of achieving success through resilience, integrity, and a commitment to ethical and socially responsible practices.

The conclusion of "The Celebration of Resilience" serves as a pivotal moment for Thabo, reinforcing his dedication to his principles and vision as he looks forward to the next stages of his journey. The celebration of Thabo's project marks not just a professional milestone but also a personal one. It is a moment of reflection on the journey that has led him here, filled with challenges overcome, lessons learned, and successes achieved.

This celebration is a crucial pause, a time to take stock before moving forward. In the midst of the celebration, Thabo takes a moment to reaffirm his commitment to the core values that have guided him: resilience, integrity, and a focus on making a positive impact. This reaffirmation is vital as it grounds him and reminds him of the principles that drive his actions and decisions. With the project's success as a launching pad, Thabo looks to the future with optimism and a sense of purpose. He is ready to embrace new challenges and opportunities, armed with the experience and confidence gained from his recent endeavours.

Thabo recognizes that his journey of personal and professional growth is ongoing. He remains open to new learnings, ready to adapt and evolve. His commitment to growth ensures that he will continue to be a dynamic and impactful leader. Thabo's story and the celebration of his resilience and integrity continue to inspire those around him. He becomes not just a leader in his field but also an agent of change, encouraging others to pursue success with a commitment to values and community.

Thabo stands at the threshold of a new path, one that promises continued growth, challenges, and opportunities. His celebration of resilience is more than a moment of triumph; it's a springboard into the future, where he will continue to lead, inspire, and make a difference, guided by the resilience and integrity that have characterized his journey so far.

The Celebration of Resilience marks a significant point in Thabo's narrative, where he not only celebrates his achievements but also renews his commitment to his values and goals. This chapter serves as a testament to the power of resilience, integrity, and continuous growth, setting the stage for the next chapter of Thabo's journey.

Thabo reflects on the lasting impact of his work and his influence as a mentor and inspiration to others, solidifying his role as a transformative figure in both his professional field and community.

In this chapter, Thabo takes a moment to reflect on the broader impact of his work, especially the landmark project in Cape Town, assessing how his commitments have reshaped not just his life but also the wider community and industry. Thabo reflects on the tangible benefits his Cape Town project has brought. He considers the advancements in technology, the improvements in community services, and the economic opportunities that have been created. These benefits are a direct result of his vision and efforts, and they affirm the positive impact of his work.

Thabo's unwavering commitment to ethical practices in his business ventures has set a new benchmark in his industry. He reflects on how this approach has influenced his peers and competitors, encouraging a shift towards more responsible and transparent business practices.

Reflecting on his community engagement, Thabo recognizes the transformation that has occurred within the Cape Town community. His initiatives have fostered a spirit of collaboration and empowerment, leading to sustainable community development. This aspect of his work brings him a deep sense of pride and accomplishment.

Thabo's innovative approach to blending technology with social impact has sparked a wave of innovation in his field. He sees how his work has inspired others to think creatively and to pursue projects that are not only profitable but also beneficial to society. This period of reflection brings Thabo a profound sense of personal fulfilment.

Knowing that his work has made a real difference gives him a feeling of satisfaction that goes beyond professional achievements. It reinforces his belief in the path he has chosen. As Thabo concludes his reflection, he is filled with a sense of gratification and purpose. The impact of his work in Cape Town and beyond is a testament to his commitment to making a positive difference.

His journey stands as a legacy of how business acumen, combined with ethical integrity and a dedication to community, can create lasting positive change. The Legacy Left Behind provides a thoughtful look at the significant and positive changes Thabo has catalysed through his work.

This reflection not only underscores the tangible benefits of his projects but also highlights the personal fulfilment and broader influence he has gained from his commitment to ethical practices, community engagement, and innovative thinking.

Thabo's legacy is examined through the lens of his unwavering commitment to professional ethics and innovation, highlighting how he has reshaped industry standards and influenced the broader business landscape. Thabo's approach to business, characterized by a strong ethical foundation, has set a new standard in his industry. He has demonstrated that it is possible to be successful in business while maintaining integrity, honesty, and a commitment to doing what is right.

This approach has challenged conventional business practices and inspired a shift towards more ethical conduct in the corporate world. Thabo has shown that balancing profitability with principles is not only possible but also desirable. His projects have been profitable, yet they have always prioritized ethical considerations and social responsibility.

This balance has become a hallmark of his work, proving that financial success does not have to come at the expense of ethical values. Thabo's innovative strategies, which seamlessly integrate technology with social impact, have influenced the way businesses approach innovation. He has inspired others to consider the broader impact of their innovations, encouraging a focus on solutions that are beneficial both commercially and socially.

Thabo's journey has inspired a new generation of leaders who admire his commitment to ethics and innovation. He has shown that leadership is not just about guiding a team to meet business goals but also about instilling values and principles that transcend the workplace. The impact of Thabo's work extends beyond his industry. His commitment to social responsibility and ethical practices has influenced other sectors, encouraging organizations to adopt more responsible and sustainable business practices.

As the section concludes, Thabo's legacy in professional ethics and innovation is firmly established. He has not only achieved commercial success but has also contributed to the evolution of business practices towards a more ethical and socially responsible approach. His legacy is one that will continue to influence the industry and inspire future leaders for years to come. Thabo's profound impact on reshaping business practices. His dedication to ethical integrity and innovative solutions that consider social impact has set new benchmarks in his industry, influencing current and future leaders to pursue success responsibly and ethically.

Thabo's influence extends beyond his immediate professional achievements, as he becomes a mentor and a source of inspiration for a new generation of professionals and entrepreneurs. Thabo's role as a mentor is deeply enriched by his own experiences.

He provides guidance and advice that is practical, relatable, and grounded in the realities of navigating the business world. His mentees benefit from his insights on overcoming challenges, ethical decision-making, and balancing professional aspirations with personal values.

Thabo's journey, marked by resilience in the face of adversity and unwavering commitment to his principles, serves as a powerful source of inspiration. His story resonates with aspiring professionals and entrepreneurs, showing them that it is possible to overcome obstacles and achieve success while maintaining integrity and ethical standards. Through his mentorship, Thabo actively fosters a new generation of leaders who are not only skilled in their professions but also conscious of their impact on society and the environment. He encourages them to think creatively, act responsibly, and lead with compassion and empathy.

Thabo advocates for ethical entrepreneurship, emphasizing the importance of building businesses that are not only profitable but also socially responsible. He instils in his mentees the understanding that true success encompasses both financial stability and positive societal impact. Thabo's mentorship empowers others to pursue their goals with confidence and clarity. He helps them to see the value in their ideas and the importance of staying true to their convictions, fostering a sense of empowerment that extends beyond the business realm.

As the section concludes, Thabo's legacy as a mentor and inspirational figure is firmly established. His influence will continue to be felt through the lives and careers of those he has mentored, perpetuating a cycle of positive impact and ethical leadership in the business world and beyond. Role as a Mentor and Inspirational Figure highlights the significant impact Thabo has had as a mentor and role model. His journey inspires a new wave of professionals and entrepreneurs, influencing them to pursue their aspirations with resilience, integrity, and a commitment to making a meaningful difference in the world.

Thabo's commitment to nurturing future leaders is showcased, highlighting his dedication to shaping the next generation of ethical and innovative professionals. Thabo dedicates a significant portion of his time to mentorship. He recognizes the value of guiding and supporting those who are at the earlier stages of their professional journeys.

His commitment to mentorship stems from a genuine desire to give back and share the wisdom he has gained from his own experiences. Thabo's mentorship is enriched by his willingness to share real-world experiences, both successes and failures. He provides practical insights and advice, helping mentees understand the complexities of the business world and how to navigate them effectively.

A key focus of Thabo's mentorship is fostering a mindset that values ethical practices and innovative thinking. He encourages his mentees to think creatively, to challenge the status quo, and to always consider the ethical implications of their decisions and actions. Thabo tailors his mentorship to the individual needs and aspirations of his mentees. He takes the time to understand their goals, strengths, and challenges, offering personalized guidance and support that helps them grow both personally and professionally.

Through his mentorship, Thabo aims to build a community of future leaders who are equipped to lead with integrity and vision. He fosters a network where these emerging leaders can connect, share ideas, and support each other, creating a ripple effect of positive change and innovation.

As the section concludes, Thabo's role in nurturing future leaders is recognized as a vital part of his legacy. His mentorship not only impacts the individuals he guides but also contributes to the broader goal of cultivating a new generation of leaders who are committed to ethical practices, innovation, and social responsibility.

The Legacy Left Behind" emphasizes Thabo's significant contribution to the development of future leaders. His active engagement in mentorship and his dedication to instilling values of ethics and innovation mark a lasting legacy, shaping the minds and careers of the next generation of industry leaders.

Thabo's influence extends beyond the tangible achievements of his career, as he continues to inspire change and innovation in his community and industry, even while reflecting on his legacy.

Thabo's journey, marked by resilience, innovation, and ethical leadership, continues to serve as a source of inspiration for many. His story, shared in various forums and platforms, motivates others to pursue their aspirations with the same determination and commitment to values.

Thabo encourages creative problem-solving in his industry, challenging others to think outside the traditional confines of business and technology. He advocates for solutions that are not only effective but also socially responsible and sustainable, inspiring a new approach to innovation.

Through his example, Thabo promotes the importance of ethical leadership. He demonstrates that success and integrity can coexist in the business world, encouraging current and future leaders to prioritize ethical considerations in their decision-making processes. Thabo's commitment to community engagement and social responsibility continues to influence his peers and colleagues. He champions the idea that businesses should play an active role in improving the communities they operate in, inspiring others to integrate social impact into their business models.

Thabo's approach to business and innovation has spurred evolution within his industry. He has shown that adopting sustainable practices, focusing on ethical operations, and considering the broader impact of business decisions can lead to lasting positive change. As this section concludes, Thabo's influence as a catalyst for positive change is evident. His legacy is not just in what he has achieved but also in how he continues to inspire and influence those around him. He remains a figure who embodies the potential for businesses to drive positive change in society and the environment.

Thabo's impact transcends his immediate accomplishments, making him a lasting figure of inspiration in his community and industry. His commitment to ethical leadership, innovation, and community engagement continues to encourage others to pursue meaningful and responsible paths in their professional lives.

The Legacy Left Behind encapsulates the enduring legacy that Thabo leaves, a legacy characterized by ethical success, resilience in the face of adversity, and a profound commitment to making a difference in the world. Thabo's legacy is defined by his success, achieved not at the expense of his principles, but in harmony with them. He has shown that integrity and professionalism can coexist and lead to achievements that are both personally fulfilling and beneficial to society. The resilience Thabo has displayed throughout his journey, overcoming challenges and turning obstacles into opportunities for growth, serves as a cornerstone of his legacy. It's a testament to his strength of character and an inspiration to others facing their own trials.

Thabo's unwavering commitment to enacting positive change, both in his industry and community, defines his legacy. He has not only implemented projects with significant social impact but has also inspired others to consider how their work can contribute to the greater good. An integral part of Thabo's legacy is the impact he has had as a mentor and role model. His guidance and the example he has set will continue to influence and shape the careers and lives of those he has mentored, perpetuating a cycle of ethical leadership and innovation.

Thabo's principles, approaches, and achievements will continue to influence and shape the industry and communities he has been a part of. His legacy is not confined to his lifetime but extends into the future, through the people and projects he has influenced. As the chapter closes, Thabo's legacy stands as a beacon of ethical success, resilience, and positive impact. It's a legacy that transcends his personal achievements, living on in the individuals he has inspired, the changes he has instigated, and the continued pursuit of excellence and responsibility in the business world.

The Legacy Left Behind beautifully summarizes the profound and lasting legacy left by Thabo. His journey, characterized by ethical leadership, resilience, and a commitment to positive change, sets a powerful example and continues to inspire and shape the paths of individuals and industries alike.

EPILOGUE: THE JOURNEY CONTINUES

In the epilogue of "Worshipers' Masks," Thabo reflects on his journey and looks towards the future, sharing his final thoughts on ambition, success, and the interconnectedness of the world.

Thabo stands at a pivotal moment in his life, reflecting on his past experiences and looking forward with optimism and wisdom to the opportunities that lie ahead. With the culmination of significant milestones in his career, Thabo looks towards the future with a sense of optimism. The challenges he has overcome and the successes he has achieved have equipped him with a hopeful outlook for what lies ahead. He sees each new day as an opportunity to continue making a difference.

The wisdom Thabo has garnered from his experiences is invaluable. He has learned about the complexities of balancing personal ambition with social responsibility, the importance of resilience in the face of adversity, and the impact of ethical leadership. These lessons will guide his future decisions and actions.

Thabo's view of his professional pursuits has evolved. He no longer sees his career as just a series of business ventures or projects but as a platform for creating wider positive change. His future endeavours are shaped by a desire to contribute meaningfully to society and the industry.

As he looks to the future, Thabo is eager to embrace opportunities that allow him to expand his impact. Whether it's through mentoring, launching new initiatives, or advocating for change, he is committed to using his skills, experience, and influence to make a difference. The lessons Thabo has learned through his journey are his guiding light. They remind him of the importance of staying true to one's values, the power of perseverance, and the impact of leading by example. These lessons shape his approach to future challenges and opportunities.

The section ends with Thabo standing at the threshold of a future filled with possibilities. He is ready to take on new challenges, to explore new horizons, and to continue his journey of growth and impact. His optimism and wisdom, forged through his experiences, illuminate his path forward.

"Looking Towards the Future" in "The Journey Continues" encapsulates Thabo's optimistic and wise outlook as he stands ready to embrace the future. His experiences have shaped a broader perspective on his professional pursuits, highlighting his commitment to creating a lasting impact in the world.

The Journey Continues" - Redefining Success

Thabo's transformation in how he perceives and channels his ambition is explored, highlighting a shift from personal achievements to a broader, more impactful vision. Thabo's understanding of ambition has undergone a profound transformation. Where once his ambitions were focused on personal success and recognition, he now views ambition as a means to effect broader societal and global change. His goals are no longer cantered just on his own success but on creating positive impacts in the world.

For Thabo, ambition is now a tool to drive innovation, inspire others, and bring about meaningful change. He sees the potential of ambition to transform communities, uplift societies, and address significant global challenges. His ambition is aligned with his values and the desire to leave a positive legacy. Thabo's journey has taught him that true fulfilment in ambition comes not from personal accolades but from the difference he can make. His focus has shifted from achieving for the sake of personal gain to achieving for the sake of contributing to the greater good.

Thabo's evolved view of ambition also serves to inspire others. He encourages aspiring professionals and entrepreneurs to think beyond traditional notions of success and to see their ambitions as pathways to creating positive societal impact.

Thabo's ambition is now intertwined with a commitment to sustainable and ethical practices. He understands that lasting impact requires a balance of innovation, responsibility, and a long-term view of success.

As Thabo looks towards the future, his ambition, refined and purposeful, is a driving force in his continued journey. He steps forward with the intent to not only achieve but to inspire, innovate, and impact, marking a significant evolution in his understanding and application of ambition.

The Journey Continues reflects Thabo's profound shift in perspective on ambition, from a focus on personal success to a powerful tool for societal and global impact. This evolution signifies a deeper alignment of his goals with his values, emphasizing the potential of ambition to bring about meaningful and lasting change.

The Journey Continues" - Redefining Success

Thabo's journey culminates in a profound redefinition of what success means to him, moving away from conventional benchmarks to a more holistic and impactful understanding.

Thabo has come to realize that true success cannot be quantified solely by financial gain, prestigious titles, or accolades. Instead, he measures success by the positive changes he can effect in his community and the broader world. This shift reflects a deeper understanding of the impact and responsibility that come with success.

For Thabo, success now includes the tangible improvements he can make in the lives of those in his community. Whether it's through job creation, providing innovative solutions to local problems, or contributing to societal welfare, his success is intertwined with the well-being of others. Thabo views conducting his work with integrity as a key component of success. He believes that how one achieves success is as important as the achievement itself. This commitment to ethical practices and principled decision-making has become an integral part of his definition of success.

The legacy that Thabo leaves behind is a crucial aspect of his redefined success. He aspires to be remembered not just for what he achieved but for how he influenced others, the values he espoused, and the positive changes he initiated. His legacy is about the lasting impact of his actions and ideas. Success, in Thabo's perspective, is fundamentally about making a meaningful difference. It's about using one's skills, resources, and position to contribute positively to society and the environment, creating a ripple effect of positive change.

As Thabo continues his journey, his redefined concept of success guides his decisions and actions. This new definition, focusing on community impact, integrity, and legacy, transforms his pursuit of success into a purposeful endeavour that seeks to benefit not just himself but the world at large. "Redefining Success" in the epilogue "The Journey Continues" captures Thabo's evolved understanding of success, one that transcends traditional measures and is deeply rooted in making a meaningful difference in the community and the world. This redefinition reflects a mature and holistic view of success, emphasizing the importance of impact, integrity, and legacy.

The Journey Continues" - Understanding The Interconnectedness Of The World

Thabo delves into the realization of how deeply interconnected the world is and how each individual's actions contribute to the larger narrative of humanity. Thabo reflects on how each of his decisions and actions, much like those of every individual, weaves into the vast tapestry of global events and consequences. He understands that his journey, while personal, is part of a much larger story of human endeavour and experience.

He acknowledges that the impact of his work extends beyond his immediate environment. His projects, particularly those focusing on sustainability and social responsibility, have implications that resonate on a global scale, contributing to broader conversations about environmental stewardship and ethical business practices. Thabo contemplates the ripple effect of individual actions. He sees how choices made in one part of the world can affect people and environments far away. This understanding reinforces his commitment to making decisions that are not only beneficial locally but also considerate of their global implications.

With this understanding of interconnectedness, Thabo feels a heightened sense of global responsibility. He is more conscious of his role as a global citizen and is motivated to contribute positively to the world, not just through his professional endeavours but also in his personal life. Thabo's insights into the interconnectedness of the world influence others around him. He encourages his colleagues, mentees, and peers to recognize their place in the global community and to act in ways that contribute positively to the world at large.

As this section concludes, Thabo embraces the concept of global interconnectedness with a sense of humility and responsibility. He moves forward with a renewed commitment to actions that acknowledge and respect the intricate web of connections that bind the world together.

"Understanding the Interconnectedness of the World" in the epilogue "The Journey Continues" highlights Thabo's deepened understanding of how individual actions are part of a larger global context. This realization brings a renewed sense of responsibility and a commitment to making decisions that positively impact the global community, reinforcing the significance of global interconnectedness in shaping our collective future.

The Journey Continues" - The Responsibility of Influence

Thabo grapples with the realization of his growing influence and the accompanying responsibility, shaping his approach as he moves forward. Thabo comes to a profound understanding of the extent of his influence. He recognizes that his decisions, actions, and leadership style have the power to inspire and shape the perspectives and actions of others, both within his immediate circle and beyond. With this recognition, Thabo embraces his role as an influencer with a renewed sense of responsibility. He is mindful of the impact his words and deeds have on others and is committed to using his influence positively, to inspire, guide, and encourage.

Thabo's approach to leadership evolves to one that is even more conscious of setting a positive example. He understands that his behaviour and choices can serve as a model for others, and he strives to lead in a way that exemplifies the values and principles he stands for. This newfound awareness influences Thabo's decision-making process. He considers not just the immediate outcomes of his decisions but also their broader implications on those who look up to him and the messages they convey about his values and priorities.

Thabo uses his influence to drive positive change in his industry and community. He advocates for ethical practices, social responsibility, and innovation that benefits society, hoping to inspire others in positions of influence to do the same. As this section concludes, Thabo steps into the future as a thoughtful influencer, acutely aware of the responsibility that comes with his growing impact. He moves forward with the intention to use his influence to create a positive ripple effect, contributing to a better world through his actions and leadership. The Journey Continues" emphasizes Thabo's conscious embrace of his role as an influencer. His understanding of the impact of his actions and decisions marks a significant shift in his approach, highlighting his commitment to responsible and positive leadership that extends beyond his immediate scope of work.

The Journey Continues" - Embracing the Journey Ahead

The Journey Continues" culminates with Thabo poised to embark on the next phase of his life, armed with a wealth of experience and a renewed perspective on his role in the world. Thabo stands at this pivotal moment with a mature and balanced understanding of ambition and success. His experiences have taught him that true ambition is about creating value and making a difference, and success is measured not just in personal achievements but in the positive impact made on the world.

Thabo's awareness of the interconnectedness of the world influences his approach to the future. He is cognizant of how his actions can affect others far beyond his immediate environment and is motivated to make decisions that are beneficial on a global scale. As he looks ahead, Thabo is committed to continuing his journey of making a meaningful difference. He remains dedicated to his goals of driving ethical business practices, fostering innovation, and contributing to societal progress. Thabo's journey itself becomes a testament to the power of resilience, integrity, and purposeful ambition. He stands as a living example of how facing challenges with determination and adhering to one's principles can lead to profound personal and professional fulfilment.

Embracing the future with optimism, Thabo is ready to take on new challenges and opportunities. He steps forward with the confidence of someone who has navigated numerous storms, yet retains the eagerness to learn, grow, and explore new possibilities. As "The Journey Continues" draws to a close, Thabo's story leaves a lasting impression of inspiration and insight. He steps into the future not just as a successful individual but as a visionary leader, a mentor, and an agent of change, ready to continue his impactful journey in an ever-evolving world.

The conclusion of the epilogue "The Journey Continues" encapsulates Thabo's readiness to embark on the next chapter of his life, highlighting his evolved understanding of ambition, success, and his interconnected role in the world. His story stands as an inspiring narrative, demonstrating the profound impact of resilience, integrity, and purpose-driven ambition.

~~~~~~~~~~~~~~~~~~~~**END**~~~~~~~~~~~~~~~~~~~~~
~~~~~~~~~~~~~~~~~~~~

THANK YOU, LETTER, FROM THE AUTHOR

Dear Readers,

As I write this thank-you note, my heart is filled with a myriad of emotions: gratitude, hope, and a touch of nervousness. Publishing "Worshipers' Masks: The Hidden Faces of Success
" has been an enlightening journey, and the fact that you chose to read it fills me with immense gratitude.

First and foremost, I want to thank you for investing your time in reading this book. Time is the most valuable commodity we have, and the fact that you decided to spend some of it exploring these pages means the world to me. I hope the information, insights, and discussions presented have given you a better understanding of the complex, often disturbing world of social media and its impact on our lives and society.

Thank you to all the my family, my friends, experts, psychologists, social media gurus, and everyday people who shared their life journey stories, experiences and insights with me during my journey for this book. Your contributions have been invaluable. I also want to extend my appreciation to friends and family who provided emotional support and constructive criticism throughout the writing process.

A special thanks to the team of editors, designers, and marketers who believed in the vision of this book and worked tirelessly to make it a reality. Without your skills and dedication, this project would have remained a mere idea.

While the book tackles uncomfortable truths and exposes the dark underbelly of our digital lives, it is my belief that knowledge is the first step toward change. I hope that after reading this, you feel empowered to make that change, to speak up, and to protect not just yourself but also those who might not have a voice.

As you navigate your way through the maze of social media, particularly on platforms like X, keep in mind that every click, every share, every comment is a choice that contributes to the larger narrative. Let's strive to make those choices reflect our better selves.

I look forward to hearing your thoughts, criticisms, and suggestions as they will only aid in enriching this ongoing conversation. My wish is that this book acts as a catalyst for informed dialogue and constructive change.

Thank you once again for embarking on this journey with me. Your support has made all the difference.

Warm regards,

Onesimus Malatji